The Sing Song Child

...a love story

Mike Casper

The Sing Song Child, a love story
Mike Casper

© 2015 Mike Casper, ALL RIGHTS RESERVED
ISBN-13: 978-0-9905144-0-4 (Paperback edition)
ISBN-13: 978-0-9905144-1-1 (eBook edition)

Sing Song Publishing
2588 El Camino Real Suite F165 Carlsbad, Ca. 92008
Please direct web queries to *mike.casper@gmail.com*

Don't tell me the sky's
the limit when
there are footprints on the moon.

-anonymous

Chapter One

THE YEAR 1574 Anno Domini
IN THE SOVEREIGN COUNTRY OF
TIERARY, NESTLED BETWEEN FRANCE
AND THE NETHERLANDS.

Around a washed out bend in the road came a quickly moving formation of armed riders escorting a horse and carriage. The carriage hit a muddy rut in a particularly rough stretch and lurched to the side. The occupants, a boy and a middle aged woman, were tossed about; the boy bounced hard off the sidewall. The vehicle lurched again, prompting the driver to slow the carriage almost to a crawl and the driver to call back, "Sorry."

A woman's voice replied, "Andrew and I are fine, Penn, we're used to the bumps." As the passengers steadied themselves, movement out the window drew the boy's attention to a peasant family collecting the remaining potatoes of the season. A girl his age looked toward the carriage and rubbed away a splotch of dirt from her nose.

Barefoot, except for rags tied around her feet and desperately thin, she stood and waved to the boy. Their eyes locked, she felt a flutter in her heart. He smiled and waved back. Her stepfather's sharp, "Sophie" broke her gaze and she turned away. She drew her threadbare shawl tighter around her shoulders and blew into her hands. In a reedy voice she said out loud to herself, "A carriage and smart looking lad my age, too. Good for him."

She looked at the heavens. Fog had coated the landscape much of the day but now, as evening fell, the sky overhead looked like the rough woolen blanket on her straw mattress. She could almost see bedbugs.

Her shoulders sagged a little and a tear trickled down her grimy face. She scratched an itch. "Yet, where's the fairness, Lord? He gets a carriage and I get potatoes and bugs. Why?" As if in response to her plea, for one spectacular moment the entire bottom of the cloud layer burst forth in a blaze of pink, purple and orange, giving life and color to the land. She smiled to herself, murmured a quiet 'thank you' and started digging with her worn hand-me-down potato shovel. It slid underneath a potato then hit something else, something hard and unyielding. The blade of her shovel sheared off and its shaft snapped in two.

Frustrated, she squatted and tugged hard at the defiant potato. To her surprise, the tuber shot out of the earth and the girl sat down hard. Red-faced, she rubbed her bum and turned towards the boy in the carriage. To her immense relief she could somehow tell he was smiling with her misfortune, not at her. Sophie smiled back then dug in the hole to retrieve the rest of her shovel. She partially unearthed what broke her tool: the tip of a large, smooth white rock. Alongside the stone was a palm sized shard of reddish pottery and a round disk of grey clay. There was an unusual black line painted on the pottery and, curious, she unearthed the fragments. A well placed gob of spit rubbed on the pottery exposed the image of a man with a prominent nose reclining on a couch.

She glanced over her shoulder at Stepfather, who by now had a tankard of ale in his hand and was sitting in the back of their battered wagon. She again peeked back at him then looked into the hole and moved more dirt. She could see more disks and a larger piece of pottery. She pocketed the shard and one of the disks then filled in the hole.

Just then her mother called, "Sophie, that's enough for one day. Let's go home." Sighing, she rose and gathered her potatoes. She missed her daddy. Mother had re-married shortly after his death a year ago, for she had children to protect and feed. Unlike her real father, the new head of the house would become angry if she lingered in the field. Nice to her at first, Stepfather had turned out to be a harsh man, especially when he had been drinking a lot of ale. She had learned to not anger him, and to dodge his efforts to catch her alone. That he might succeed one day made molten bile rise in her throat and revulsion shake her frame. She would have to stay quiet in the shadows till after he went to sleep tonight and then hide in her safe place behind Mother's spinning wheel. And pray he did not wake up.

As Sophie was walking back to rejoin her family, on a whim she turned around and tossed the broken shaft of her now unusable shovel on the ground close to where she had found the fragments. From across the field a partridge's raspy call made her smile and she tried to trick the bird to reply with her own call as Daddy had taught her. Success.

Another glance at the retreating carriage confirmed the handsome lad was still looking at her. They smiled, her heart leaped again, and then they both turned away.

The carriage crested a rise and the boy looked back at the shrinking figure in the field. In the valley ahead was the high protective wall of their destination, Whittleford town. The carriage picked up speed and after a moment the girl was gone.

The carriage's other passenger, Crestina, a plump, flaxen-haired nanny leaned forward. "Andrew, pay attention my boy. You've let your blankets fall away and the coverlet is a family heirloom." She reached down and tucked a woven woolen blanket around the boy's spindly legs, then added a green, blue, and red embroidered silk coverlet on top. "There, Andrew, as good as new." She leaned closer and looked at him with a bit of alarm. "Are you feeling okay? Andrew? I know. Shall we sing a song? I haven't heard you sing for hours."

Andrew's face was flushed, his pulse raced and his mouth was dry. He felt stronger and more vital than ever before. As he tried to commit every detail about the peasant girl to memory, he was aware of a great yearning in the pit of his belly. Tears trickled down his cheek as he looked with frustration and disgust at his useless legs. Yet again he begged God to let him skip and jump and run about in the sunlight as a normal boy. "A chance, Lord, please, just a tiny hope of being like them."

Just then the leader of the armed men called back, "Whittleford town in sight."

Andrew and Crestina leaned out their windows; she to see the city ahead but Andrew looking backward for the girl with the dirty face and pretty eyes.

The carriage and entourage passed safely through the high gates of Whittleford. With friendly waves, the armed escorts wheeled their horses away towards the stables. The carriage slowed to an easy pace as it navigated busy cobblestoned streets. They passed a small but bustling marketplace where a dozen or so merchants were concluding their business day, hoping for a last minute sale. Dodging traffic and piles of fresh horse dung, a boy about half Andrew's age carried a covey of quail in a woven wicker basket while leading a fat pig twice his size by a leather leash. The next morning would end badly for the pig, but well for patrons of a local tavern.

Enthralled by the city, Andrew's attention was brought back upon himself by a strange, hot feeling that started in his lower back, spiraled down his legs, then traveled up his torso. His hands and feet started to tingle. For the first time in his life the toes on his right foot, then his left, responded ever so slightly to his command. The heat spiraled up his neck to the top of his head; his throat burned as if he had eaten a chili pepper. He tried but was unable to utter a sound. Then the feeling faded as suddenly as it had come.

He wiggled a big toe and said a silent, fervent "Thank you" to God.

The carriage came to a brief stop and Andrew looked out the window towards the city, trying to understand what had happened. He noticed a white dove watching him from its perch on the canvas roof of an adjacent surrey. It cooed twice and, with a flap of its wings, disappeared over the rooftops.

Smiling his lopsided smile, his heart soaring alongside the dove, with great effort he stroked a two-week-old raggedy line of rough blonde hairs sprouting on his upper lip.

Crestina noticed Andrew's grin and smiled as she smoothed his blanket. She squeezed his hand. "We're almost there, Andrew. Just a little while longer and we'll be there." He squeezed back ever so slightly but she did not notice. In his slow and hesitating speech, he said, "Kesy, ou illse. Ill alk. Omeay."

Crestina smiled sadly, "Yes, you will walk. Someday." She kissed his forehead and pointed out his window, "Oh look, Andrew, the city is always so beautiful in the evening."

Chapter Two
In the Alleyway

*I*t was a job best done with three arms; the lamplighter had but one. The other had been lost in battle. He stretched up high on a rickety ladder and lit his last tallow of the evening. A carriage approached at an easy pace. The lamplighter turned and grinned as he recognized the driver, a former comrade-in-arms. He blew out his wick and put it in his pocket. At great peril to himself, he pivoted on a rung of the ladder and saluted his friend, Penn the Scot.

Penn, an enormous man, smiled back, then stood at the driver's seat. In one motion he pushed back his tri-corner hat and returned the salute. He held his stance as the wagon turned down an alley between a series of large, rambling stone buildings. Only when the lamplighter was no longer in sight did he sit down to resume his duties.

The clomping of the horses' hooves echoed off the stone walls and mixed with the sounds of a child's tin horn and singing, coming from the carriage.

The clamor woke a black cat napping in its den on the second floor of an adjacent building. As the wagon stopped in front of a heavy wooden door, the feline emerged, flicked its white tipped tail and looked on with rapt attention.

Penn jumped down from his perch and knocked on the door. He removed his hat, revealing short, silvery hair and a jagged scar on the back of his head. A small viewing panel recessed into the wall near the door slid open. He exchanged a few quiet words with someone inside. After a moment the door swung open with a creaking groan.

The cat stood, yawned, arched his back in a luxuriant stretch and disappeared into the shadows.

With surprising gentleness for a man his size, Penn escorted Crestina into the building. He returned to the wagon for a coverlet-and-blanket-wrapped Andrew. He made a third trip for a wicker chair with two spindly wheels attached on each side. As he turned and bid goodbye, a small black shape slipped unnoticed between his feet and into the building.

Chapter Three
Trouble

Sophie added a small log to the dying fire and glanced around her family's home. Their landowner, Earl of Woolsley, despised for his longstanding practice of garnishing far more than the normal ten percent tithe of his land's yield, had stopped by to assess his holdings. He and his aide-de-camp were drinking ale with Stepfather.

It was not uncommon for land-owners to stay at their peasants' homes while inspecting their land, and it looked like that was to happen tonight. The peasants were expected to provide meals and safe lodging. Their guest looked at her with an unholy interest, his eyes and face feral and sinister. She shrank back into the shadows. It was whispered that the earl had a dark taste for girls not quite to the age of womanhood. A deep, ugly, crimson scar traversing his face, and half a missing ear bore testimony that one girl's father had fought for his daughter's honor.

Her stomach growled out loud; the earl had eaten most of their family's meager meal and was preparing for sleep. Stepfather, now clearly intoxicated, was cleaning their shovels for the next day's use, for tools were precious to those with little. He slurred, "Sophie, where's your digging tool?" She looked down and away. How foolish to have left the shaft in the field she thought grimly. Now I'm really going to catch it.

Stepfather held up the broken blade and roared, perhaps out of indignation but also maybe to show off for his guest. "Have you broken another, you-good-for-nothing miserable whelp? Where's the shaft? Now I must carve another *and* mend the blade again. Don't you know how busy I am? I've half a mind to clout you on your ears."

As before, her mother quickly moved to intervene on her behalf but this time Stepfather was having none of it. His rage rising, he pushed his wife aside roughly. "You have, haven't you, Sophie. You've broken it again. That's the third time this season. Have I not told you to take care of my tools?" He raised his fist as if to strike her and snarled, "No. I'm tired of supporting you, child. You're sickly and not particularly pretty or smart and I will not have you living in my home any longer. Out with you now. Be gone. I disown you as my stepdaughter."

Mother gasped and tried to talk sense into Stepfather but he smacked her hard with the back of his hand and grabbed Sophie by the arm. Roughly, he dragged her to the door. This time was different somehow, and she started twisting in his grasp, crying and pleading, "I can find it. I know where it is, Stepfather. It broke. It was worn out. I can fix it. Please let me go look. Don't kick me out. Please. I'll die out there."

He let out a great belch and his breath stank of sour ale, onions, and decayed teeth. He screamed, "Out of my house with you now, vermin child. I'm done with you."

With an enormous heave he threw her out into the night and she fell on the dirt, barely missing a puddle of muck. A few moments later the door opened, and her shawl landed on the ground in front of her feet. She could hear her brother and stepsisters yelling at the brute, and then the sick sound of what she guessed was her brother Rhys hitting the heavy wooden table. Mother's weeping mixed with the earl's rising laughter. Then the house went silent.

Chapter Four
Preparations

As Alphonse smoothed the last tiny crinkle from his black silk vest he stepped back to examine himself in the long gilt-frame mirror at the Whittleford Inn. It revealed a smattering of gray in his longish brown hair and a fading scar on his left cheek. He appraised himself with a critical eye and smiled. "Not too bad, old chap. You've somehow escaped the ravages of age."

"Yes, you *do* look marvelous, my dear," a sweet voice murmured from behind. "I must say, I fall in love with you again each time you wear your formal sash and cloak. You look so, dignified—so – so *distinguished*."

Alphonse patted a battered flintlock pistol at his hip. "See, Chantal, I've even polished the blunderbuss Admiral Pennington gave me to commemorate my taking command of the *Benadene*."

Chantal giggled and gave him a mock salute. "The *Benadene*, my captain? I wish that ship was still afloat. I wonder where it would be today. You know, I remember that day so long ago. Were we wedded only three years? I was so proud of you. I always love it when you wear your pistol and saber. And your decorations and medals. They make you look quite dashing, and a bit menacing, don't you think?"

Alphonse made an adjustment to his tunic then turned to face her. "Dashing? You flatter me. Menacing? Ha. I so love your sense of humor. I was devastated when **the** *'Bene'* went down in the hurricane off Puerto Rico. I remember those three years of patrols all too well. It could have been me in that storm. Praise God, somehow almost all hands saved, I think. She was a good ship." Alphonse's voice trailed off and he unconsciously kneaded a long scar on his lower back. "But I'm glad I was assigned to shore duty after I was hurt."

During his last voyage, Alphonse had battled the notorious pirate, Jastin, and his ship, the *Oscuro Suerte*. During an exchange of cannon fire, an incoming twenty-pound ball had blown a large chunk of the *Bene's* railing on Alphonse and two seamen. Bloodied, Alphonse had gathered his wits and fought on, his crew ultimately boarding the pirate ship and defeating them in hand-to-hand combat.

Jastin and his first mate had managed to escape in a small, fast boat. As the first mate taunted and jeered the victors, the pirate captain stood in the stern of the vessel and mockingly saluted Alphonse with Alphonse's own sword. Enraged, Alphonse had found a rifle, taken careful aim and fired. The ball had struck the pirate captain a devastating blow just below the kneecap of his left leg.

During his long recuperation, the pirate declared himself a changed man. He bribed the French king for a pardon, learned to walk with a wooden peg and was appointed mayor of Hervochoné, a notorious pirate haven on Monserrat. Jastin ruled the city with an iron fist and before long had cleaned out the riffraff and created a respectable reputation for himself.

But he was seldom seen without Alphonse's sword in hand.

Alphonse continued in a more serious tone. "I wore my weapons to defend country and King. But, my sweet, sweet, darling Chantal, when I fought, I fought only for you." He added, "And our children. And I'll do it again if I must."

With a wink, Alphonse took her into his arms and the two embraced. She gently pushed him back just a bit. "Careful, don't muss my hair my darling. This is the biggest event of the year and I want to look my best for you."

Chantal ran a finger over the scar on his cheek, lightly. She continued, "I would hope you need not place yourself in harm's way for me again, my love. I can handle myself, but I *do* feel protected and secure when we're together."

Alphonse chuckled. "I hope not either. But I would in a moment. And I know you can protect yourself as well. You're carrying your blade this evening, aren't you?"

She nodded. "Always, my captain. Always. And more."

Alphonse's hand dropped to his inside jacket pocket for the official envelope it held. The Palace had asked loyal and trusted officers to bring their weapons, in primed and ready to use condition. There were strong rumors that a band of outlaws and brigands were planning to rob those attending the event and the King's Guard wanted to meet their threat with overwhelming force.

"But enough about such talk," he smiled. "You look fabulous, Chantal." He took a slight step back and held his wife at arm's length. "You are simply becoming more exquisite with the passage of time. I thank the Lord for blessing me with such a wonderful wife for all these years."

Almost a head shorter and four years younger, Chantal pretended to primp and preen and both shared a brief chuckle. Her emerald eyes sparkled as she brushed a strand of her auburn hair back into place.

They had met at a stuffy, formal dance given by a minor official of Belgium's royal house.

Alphonse, then a young and newly commissioned officer in the Royal Navy attended – under mild protest – as ordered by his commander. Chantal, fresh from university, had attended as a favor to friends.

It was Chantal who had spied Alphonse from across the ballroom. He was surrounded by a bevy of attractive young women vying for his attention. In a scandalous breach of etiquette, Chantal had crossed the dance floor mid-waltz, dodging dozens of twirling couples. Without a formal introduction she had asked Alphonse for his hand to dance. Alphonse had glanced in his commander's direction and, after seeing his quick nod and smile of approval, accepted her offer. Unknown to Chantal, Alphonse had already seen her and had asked his commanding officer to arrange a proper introduction with the captivating beauty. During their first waltz, the conductor had noticed the attraction between the two. Inspired, he exhorted his orchestra and they played their finest. After several dances even the hardest hearted society shrew had become enchanted by the couple and soon all was forgiven in that realm.

However, there was one not so happy with Alphonse's new found love. When the ball was over and the two had said reluctant farewells, a wealthy German silver merchant had dragged Chantal into his carriage and had taken off at reckless speed.

A servant alerted Alphonse. After a furious pursuit, Alphonse found the carriage halted in the middle of the road and the kidnapper quite willing to release his captive. Chantal had produced a dagger and, after slicing off one of his earlobes – and with the earnest promise of deeper cuts in far more delicate places – had persuaded her kidnapper to order the carriage stopped.

Chantal scrambled from the transport just as Alphonse had galloped up to the scene. He jumped from his horse; she from the carriage and the couple embraced briefly. Alphonse then drew his sword to engage her kidnapper. The merchant, having regained his temper, had drawn a small flintlock pistol and snuck up on the two from the other side of the carriage.

He aimed at Chantal and growled, "If I cannot have her, nobody shall." At the last moment Alphonse turned, noticed his intent and caused the shot that would have struck his beloved to go awry. The ball gouged a ragged furrow in his cheek. Alphonse then bested him in a vicious swordfight and dispatched the man with a single sword thrust to the heart as the scoundrel tried to draw another pistol.

News of the merchant's death reached his estate, where his family reacted badly. Although the dishonored trader was clearly in the wrong, his brother had vowed vengeance. Alphonse bested the brother in duel fought with swords two weeks later.

Four months after their meeting it was Alphonse who asked Chantal for her hand, this time in marriage, and soon afterward they were expecting their first child. After a few years, a total of three beautiful and smart children, Nicholas, Andre and Gabrielle, made their family complete.

Nicholas and Andre followed in their father's footsteps and, after completing University, had joined the Royal Navy. They had risen rapidly through the ranks to commands of their own, and now held positions of importance in naval bases abroad. Gabrielle became a celebrated author and spent time in London and Paris, pursuing her craft. The children had married well and now had growing families of their own.

Alphonse continued, "And not only beautiful, but creative as well. What a stroke of genius this year, designing a silken gown the same color and texture as the beautiful roses you work with. *You*, my dear, not the displays, will be the center of attention."

Chantal hugged him tight for just a moment. She pulled away, danced across the room and glanced through the large picture window down at the main thoroughfare in the center of the town square. The sky was a beautiful shade of orange and purple. She stopped, enchanted. "Hurry, darling, come see the sunset. Look at the colors."

Alphonse joined his wife in front of the window and took her hand. "To me you are even more beautiful than the most radiant of sunsets."

Chantal's eyes teared for just a moment. "And I love you too, Alphonse. My king."

The couple hugged for a long moment. Alphonse murmured, "My queen. I say, let us not be tardy for the grand entry. The displays should be just splendid this year."

She nodded in agreement and gathered her wrap. Alphonse took up his long woolen cloak and the couple went downstairs to join the festivities.

Chapter Five
The Great Hall

The frosted windows of the Whittleford Great Hall were beautifully aglow with light from many hundreds of candles. The Bottington-Downs Wax Figurine and Candle Company was hosting its annual *Festival of Light Celebration* to salute the accomplishments of their employees with a display of their finest wares. The theme of this year's celebration was *Meaningful Events and People throughout the Ages*. Milestones of the past had come alive in the beautiful displays with the exquisite creativity by dedicated wax-smiths.

Always the European social season's biggest event, dignitaries had traveled from near and far to attend. Gentlemen, resplendent in their finest apparel and chapeaus escorted ladies dressed in their finest embroidered silk and satin gowns. Excitement ran high in the joyful expectation of wonders yet to be seen. And yet the common folk, the ordinary citizens, were not forgotten in the festivities as the company had gone to great lengths to ensure everyone was invited.

A shout arose from those waiting in the chilled evening air, for the massive, iron reinforced wooden entry doors had swung open at last.

The assembly started for the door. Streaming into the great hall, affluent and common alike were greeted by a wave of scented air warmed by the many candles. Blue-suited festival guides made certain that all received programs outlining the evening's activities. Centuries ago, the queen established a system of traveling teachers who taught peasant and merchant families how to read and write. As a result, Tierary enjoyed an unusually high percentage of literate citizenry. Nevertheless, the guides checked to make sure those who could not read understood the evening's agenda.

People of varied backgrounds mingled in the large hall, each marveling at historical scenes superbly reproduced in delicate wax constructions. The display featuring Jesus Christ on the cross and his resurrection three days later had drawn a large group of admirers, many of whom were crossing themselves with tears in their eyes. Old Testament prophet Moses's Burning Bush in the desert, the reproduction of the Jewish Passover's fearsome Angel of Death, Noah's Ark, the building of the pyramids of Egypt and Hannibal's crossing of the Alps on elephants were included as well. The beautiful Cleopatra was shown holding a viper in her hand as Galileo peered through a telescope at the Heavens and Leonardo Di Vinci pondered an unfinished invention on his table. Greek King Leonidas of Sparta and his three hundred brave volunteers again faced the Persian Empire at Thermopylae while the fabled Minotaur from Greek mythology huddled in his den and the Italian explorer Cristoforo Columbi waded ashore in the New World.

Adjacent to the famed Lighthouse at Alexandria were the hanging Gardens of Babylon and Gutenberg's revolutionary printing press. Closer to home, the English Battle of Hastings was as yet undecided and Archimedes again tried to turn lead into gold. Also superbly captured in wax was the signing of the Magna Carta in 1215 by King John of England. Darker themed exhibits included the Black Death pandemic of the mid-1300's, the "Time of Trouble" influenza which had struck the modern world, and especially, Tierary in the late 900's, and the horrible Spanish Inquisition. Other, simpler displays included native flora and fauna from Tierary and routine pastoral scenes as well.

Alphonse and Chantal spied Francisco and his wife, Mirna, waving at them from across the great hall. The couples maneuvered towards each other to greet and renew old friendships. The men exchanged bear hugs; the women greetings of a more gentle nature.

Mirna, the taller and more voluptuous of the two women, was dressed in a beautiful multicolored Indian sari which accented her warm Latina skin. Her graying black hair was held back with a turquoise band. She hugged Chantal with the affection of close sisters. The ladies locked arms and, already engrossed in lively conversation spiced with laughter about Francisco, Mirna and Andrew's recent Far Eastern trip, moved out of the flow of traffic.

Francisco, tall and lanky, shook his longish graying locks and grinned at his younger friend. "Alphonse. *Que paso, mi hermano*? How are you, my brother?"

Alphonse grinned back. "Francisco. I thought you were to be in Paris or Milan addressing the monumental matters of the world, old chap. Look at you. None the worse for wear. I say, my good man, how *do* you do it?" He leaned close to Francisco and said in a hushed voice, "I received your communique only several hours ago. Excellent timing, I must add. And Penn?"

Francisco replied in a cultured accent befitting an ambassador. "Yes, well, timing is everything, isn't it? Praise God, you were told of the Festival's special importance and contacted me via swift riders. Of *course*, my friend, I had to reply so you would not worry." He lowered his voice and continued. "Penn? Our friend Penn is steady as a rock. I spoke briefly with the mayor as we made our entrance. Andrew arrived not long ago. And his wheeled chair. You, sir, are a genius for inventing such a device for him." He moved his jacket slightly aside, revealing a brace of pistols on his belt. A deadly Japanese Katana sword hung at his side. "And yes, I am prepared to help thwart any robbery attempt. Thank you for notifying me. Many of our friends are here."

He leaned back, assumed a snobbish air and with a wave of his hand continued in a louder voice, "Fortunately, this business of saving the world was but a simple matter and we hurried home to attend. We arrived just seven days ago. But look at yourself. The honorable Chief Divinity Inspector and his wife, the renowned rose cultivation expert. Such high society in my town. I suppose you are staying at the Whittleford Inn. Such trappings are not fit for your station. You and Chantal must repose with us tonight at *La Estancia*."

Alphonse raised an eyebrow. "*La Estancia*? But my good man, we are *upper crust*. We are staying at the renowned Whittleford Inn."

Francisco bowed down on one knee and removed an imaginary hat with a flourish. He continued earnestly, "We would be honored to have such important celebrities as guests."

The men paused, looked at each other, and then burst into laughter that only became louder when they fell under the disapproving stare of Chantal and Mirna.

Mirna turned to Chantal, took her by the arm. "Come, my dear. Perhaps our little boys shall regain their stature in a moment. In the meanwhile we must pretend we do not know them." Giggling, the ladies turned their backs on their husbands and walked away.

Acting somewhat chastened, the men regained their composure and hurried to their sides.

Stunned, Sophie stared at the cottage for a long moment. Perhaps after a night sleeping off his drink, Stepfather would allow her back into the family, but as fast as that thought arrived she dismissed it. It *was* different this time, and anyway, she was tired of running from him. After a while she picked up her shawl and trudged slowly toward the barn.

The couples had known each other for over three decades, the men having met when Alphonse was recovering from his wounds in Lenore, a small Tierarian seafaring town. Daily solo walks to his favorite *boulangerie* for fresh bread and cheese brought him past the Royal Confectionery's headquarters and factory in the center of the city. One day a torrential downpour forced Alphonse to seek shelter in a crowded brasserie next to the headquarters, where he found himself at the bar next to Francisco, then chief inspector for the Royal Confectionary. Over a shared carafe of excellent port wine the men discovered common interests and developed a mutual respect for each other. Regular meetings led to a solid friendship between the two couples and frequent stays at Francisco and Mirna's estate 'La Estancia'. At Mirna's urging, Francisco offered Alphonse an overseer position at the Royal Confectionery. Alphonse left the navy and, after learning the confectionary trade, had quickly risen to the position of Assistant

Chief Inspector, Francisco's right hand man. The two had then worked in close proximity for many years. Although several years Alphonse's senior, Francisco and he had become as close as brothers. The men had shared numerous adventures and had once acted as undercover sleuths to foil the theft of a shipment of sweetlollies by a gang of hooligans at the Marina. Francisco, by now referred to by everyone as "Don Francisco", had retired from the Royal Divinity thirteen years before. Alphonse was named his successor, and after a distinguished career of his own as Chief Inspector, was retiring as well.

As their husbands worked together, Chantal and Mirna also became fast friends, discovering that each had a keen interest in the culinary arts. Not only that, Mirna and Chantal shared an amazing genius for raising vegetables and flowers. Chantal had studied horticulture at University and had graduated with top honors. A Belgian earl with extensive farmlands had hired her out to oversee his holdings. Mirna had grown up in her family's large agriculture business and had learned the myriad aspects of cultivating exotic flowers, vegetables, and other plants.

Years spent at University had resulted in Mirna completing her dual studies in Science and Economics. But each had happy memories of carefree hours in the growing-houses and gardens of their youth.

The ladies had collaborated on the development of a new genus of flower – roses that bloom their sweet pink, bright yellow, orange and dusky red beauty with the onset of the deep snows in bleakest mid-winter. With great affection, the roses, nicknamed "Torries" by the residents of Vittoria where they were first planted, soon flourished throughout the land. After a few seasons, winter had become a captivatingly beautiful time greatly anticipated by the citizens of Tierary. Earlier in the year, Snorffleham Palace had been so impressed by the country's transformation that the two were honored by the crown in a special ceremony and were declared to be "Living Treasures of the Realm."

When the friends had been reacquainted, they moved ever so slowly through the displays, savoring their beauty and discussing their implications in world history. Time passed quickly as the four discussed, deliberated and savored each exhibit. Chantal and Mirna were so caught up in the moment that they did not notice the other attendees, directed by the festival guides, quietly streaming toward a corridor far ahead.

Only after they turned down the last aisle did Chantal notice the crowd had thinned, leaving them almost the only people remaining in the Great Hall. With a hint of humor mixed with concern she said to the men, "My dear gentlemen, why is the hall almost empty? Have we been so caught up in ourselves that we have lost track of time and been closed in?"

Francisco smiled, shrugged but remained silent.

"Yes, Chantal," Mirna agreed, "It is as if there is something yet to happen. The atmosphere seems to be heavy with *anticipation*."

"Hmmmm. Yes, indeed, Mirna," Alphonse observed, and motioned to a long candlelit corridor. "What's the sign on the wall say? *Special Exhibit*? I say, how could we have overlooked that before? Let's go investigate, then."

Chapter Six
Surprise

As they emerged from the passageway, the two couples entered a huge room so tightly crowded with people that the opposite side could not be seen. On cue, a single peal from a shining silver bell rang out. As the two couples moved toward the middle of the room, the crowd parted in front of them and closed behind when they had passed.

Chantal and Mirna moved closer, too, and reached for the reassurance of their husbands' hands, who also offered their arms in escort.

As the four walked slowly through the assembly toward the middle of the chamber, someone in the back of the crowd shouted "Bravo, Chantal. Bravo, Mirna."

At once, the rest of the crowd joined in, filling the room with the reverberation of hands and voices in joyful acclaim. When the couples emerged from the crowd into the middle of the room, the ladies gasped with surprise.

In the center was a spectacular, life-sized wax display depicting Chantal and Mirna being honored by the king and queen. Arrayed behind and around the four figures were several dozen multicolored waxen roses, each a small, burning, delicately scented candle.

The mayor of Whittleford stepped forward and raised his hands to quiet the crowd. "Ladies and gentlemen, hundreds of years ago, while Tierary was still an English colony and the sickness from the Steblen devastated the English empire, our celebrated statesman, Sir Jordan, visited the English throne and negotiated our country's independence while establishing close economic and societal ties with our mother land. Peoples from all nations are welcome to find our shores and legally become productive citizens here. Tierary has prospered greatly and has grown into a mighty and benevolent country. Yet some citizens have advanced Tierary more than others, which is truly why we are gathered here this evening."

He paused and slowly turned to face Chantal and Mirna. "We have a special guest in attendance. Prince Mark, if you would please."

A gasp arose from the crowd as Prince Mark, first-born son of the king and queen, entered the room and strode towards the center. The prince's tunic and fancy embroidered Tierarian royal crest on his cloak were stitched with thread made of real gold, which flashed in the light of the many candles. Accompanying the prince were seventy soldiers from the King's Guard. Immediately the crowd parted and then closed behind the group. Everyone went to one knee in deference to the Crown. The mayor, Alphonse, Francisco, Chantal and Mirna also went to one knee, heads bowed.

A captain in the King's Guard said in a deep voice, "All rise," and the crowd stood. Most hadn't seen royalty this close before and there was a low buzzing as the crowd discussed this turn of events.

The prince greeted the two couples, then addressed the crowd. "May I present to you 'The Mothers of the Torrie Rose.'"

A shout went up from the crowd and sustained applause echoed throughout the room. It subsided and he continued, "My parents, our beloved King Adam and Queen Annalisa, have decreed that this celebration, in the Year of Our Lord, 1574, to be called forever more, 'The Year of the Torrie Rose'."

Rousing cheers for Chantal and Mirna broke out from the crowd.

The prince started to raise his hands again but a famous opera singer in the front row started singing the Tierarian national anthem. After she completed the first stanza everyone joined hands and sang along, followed by more hand clapping, cheers and whistles.

Again the prince raised his hands. "Ladies and Gentlemen, thank you for attending this wonderful event." The crowd erupted in applause.

The prince continued when the crowd had quieted down. "Since England granted us our independence so many years ago we have maintained a close relationship with our mother country. England has the Crown Jewels but Tierary has Chantal and Mirna. So, as a small token of our appreciation, from the citizens of Tierary... ."

A little boy and girl, each holding two long, slim, highly polished mahogany boxes emerged from the crowd and offered them to the prince. He opened each box and presented Chantal then Mirna with a single, long-stemmed Torrie Rose, exquisitely wrought from the finest gold in the land. Cradling each beauty was a multicolored silken cloth exactly matching the colors of their roses. With a congratulatory kiss on Chantal and Mirna's cheek, the prince raised his hands to quiet the crowd.

"Lastly, for now and forever, ladies and gentlemen, may I present to you the Mothers of the Torrie Rose, in the *Year* of the Torrie Rose."

Amid cheers, the prince stepped back and applauded the ladies as well. A loud scuffle broke out in the passageway leading from the Great Hall; for a few moments each guard and trusted subjects like Francisco and Alphonse were on the alert. A formation of guards surrounded the prince but the hubbub was just a branded pickpocket caught in the act and quickly apprehended. Justice for this second-time offender would be swift and brutal.

A trusted officer approached and whispered something in the prince's ear. After a few moments the prince cleared his throat, looked around the room and announced, "Fellow citizens, there were rumors of a possible attack on this celebration by a collection of thieves, scoundrels and ruffians." The crowd reacted nervously. "Members of the King's Guard have captured the leader of the group and we are satisfied that there is no longer any threat." He smiled, "Carry on and enjoy the festivities." A roar of approval came from his subjects, and with that the prince waved and exited the building.

Only the two couples remained in front of the display. Alphonse and Francisco also took several steps backward. Overwhelmed at the tribute and too stunned for words, the ladies stood together in front of the admiring crowd. Someone started clapping and in a second so was everyone else. The ovation lasted several minutes. Alphonse stepped forward and handed a teary-eyed Chantal his clean linen handkerchief. Francisco did the same for Mirna.

Finally, both men held up their hands to silence the crowd. Alphonse said, "I say, it seems that we have taken the 'Mothers of the Torrie Rose' quite by surprise." The crowd laughed and cheered for the women. He continued, "Friends, thank you for your kindness and assistance. Perhaps the ladies would like to make a bit of a speech –" The rest of his sentence was drowned out with more applause and hand clapping.

Someone in the back said something funny, eliciting more laughter.

Francisco spoke up. "*Amigos y amigas*, you have bestowed quite an honor on *las Señoras*. Perhaps another round of approval would be in order. Yes?" This time the ovation lasted several more minutes than the first.

Mirna was the first to regain her wits. "Thank you. Thank you all. How beautiful. The Lord gave us the inspiration and we did it for you."

Chantal echoed her friend. "Yes, for you. Praise God. And thank you all. This is quite an honor. You are too kind, too kind indeed." Both women drew their husbands close. In between hugs, the women scolded the happy fellows for concealing the display and tribute.

A familiar honking sound came from a sturdy wooden viewing platform overlooking the scene. Mirna looked up to see Andrew, their eleven-year-old son, clapping and honking his shiny brass horn. Unable to use his hands, Andrew squeezed the rubber bulbous end between his wrists. The youth was sitting in his wheelchair. Perched on his shoulder was a black cat with a white-tipped tail. Mirna waved, and Andrew responded with a lopsided grin and honk. With obvious affection, the cat rubbed its face on the boy's face, and then wrapped around the back of his neck. Through bright yellow eyes it peered out at the revelry, mewing softly.

Eyes welling with emotion, Mirna turned to her husband and said, "Oh, Francisco, thank you for having Andrew here to share this moment." A tear rolled down her cheek. "And it seems as if we have a new member of the family. Let us go to join him and meet his new friend."

With that, they slowly worked their way through the congratulatory crowd and the recently expanded little family became complete once again.

Andrew had come to live with Francisco and Mirna as a two-month-old infant eleven years before. When the boy was just days old, a severe bout of influenza similar to a lethal episode five centuries prior had swept the region, mostly affecting the weak, the very old, and small children. Many had died, including his mother. The illness had stricken Andrew, sparing his life but rendering him unable to walk, speak coherently, or manipulate objects with his hands. The influenza of old had been known to recur in its youngest victims about twelve years after they became sick. Its first manifestation then was a dry cough quickly followed by fever and death. While there was no known cure, physicians and self-proclaimed "healers" had used potions of lead and mercury, bloodletting, voodoo and even exorcism to treat the illness. Success was almost unheard of.

Happily, the virus had not affected the boy's intellect. Others were not so fortunate.

Somehow unable to have children of their own, Francisco and Mirna had adopted the child from the local orphanage with the knowledge that their adopted son would probably not live to see his thirteenth birthday. Alphonse and Chantal had helped care for the baby and indeed were quite helpful due to their experiences raising their own children.

Despite these handicaps Andrew somehow radiated an obvious, gentle-spirited love for life and had the delightful habit of humming snippets of songs that he had heard at home and school. This invariably brightened even the gloomiest day of those within earshot.

The two couples shared a special nickname for Andrew: the Sing Song Child.

During his frequent visits, as evening was upon them, Alphonse would sit in a chair for hours with the boy in his lap, telling thrilling and slightly embellished tales of his time at sea and of people in strange, faraway lands. However, Andrew's favorite time was when his uncle Alphonse would read the Bible aloud by candlelight, in front of the hearth. Once, Alphonse read First Corinthians Chapter 15, pointing out God's promise of a perfect body free from the imperfections of his present one when believers who accept Jesus's salvation die and go to Heaven.

"Andrew, you will have a new body someday, one that can dance and run and jump and perhaps even fly. Would you like that? Yes? Me, too. I cannot do all that I used to do and I am reminded that eventually I will pass away. Not today or tomorrow I hope, but you never know what the future brings. And you, my boy, will be able to sing like a bird in Heaven, too. You will worship God with the angels on streets paved with gold." He chuckled. "Gold. Imagine, people fight over gold here on Earth. Nations fight wars over the metal but in Heaven it's so common the streets are paved with it. You will experience all the wonders and joy of Heaven and be with Jesus forever. I know you cannot do these things now, but you will in the future. A new body. Someday, youngster, someday. This is your glorious promise from God right here in the bible."

Andrew had protested, "Ut io Afons ve un ow. I ealy oo."

His reply had brought tears to Alphonse's eyes, prompting the elder to lay aside his Bible and hug the boy tightly. "Yes, yes of course you have one now, Andrew. Your body is fine as God gave it to you. But you will get a new one in Heaven. God says so."

Andrew, tears welling up in his eyes, shook his head, and then took Alphonse's hand in his own. He laid his head on Alphonse's chest underneath his chin and softly hummed a gentle, nameless melody. In the deepest part of his heart, Alphonse knew that somehow this little tune was special, as if it were but a few tiny notes of a majestic angelic symphony. His anguish for the Sing Song Child melted, replaced instead by acceptance, love and the knowledge that the bible is never wrong.

Presently, Alphonse and Chantal rejoined their friends and the couple shared a loving hug with Andrew. Alphonse asked Andrew the name of his new pet.

With his usual great effort, the boy replied in his squeaky voice, "Ren, io Afons, Ren. Ike uar hma Ren oo." Mirna exclaimed, "Ren. Oh, you mean *Friend*. What a great name for your kitty, Andrew. Yes, like Tio Alphonse is your friend too." Andrew continued, "Ren eh Ren oo ehdy. Ren eh goo kiey. Ren mah goo Ren. Ren uvs Esu ike Aruu uvs Esu. Ren ode Aruu." Everyone laughed as Alphonse responded, "Yes, Ren is everybody's friend now, too. Ren told you he loves Jesus? Now, that's one smart kitty."

For several minutes Ren became the center of attention and responded with a sweet purring sound that endeared him to his new family.

Chantal and Mirna showed their golden roses to the boy, who pretended that the gifts gave off the most wonderful aroma. Alphonse made a small gold coin disappear from his hands, only to make a much larger one reappear from behind the astonished Andrew's ear. Crestina asked if Alphonse could make a diamond do the same and everyone enjoyed a good chuckle.

In the barn, Brutus the Billy Goat baaahed and softly nuzzled the girl's leg. He usually tried to head butt her when she came to milk the goats each morning and she scratched his head between his horns in gratitude. He nuzzled her leg again as if comforting her. She threw her arms around the wooly animal and started to cry. "Oh Brutus, my world has been tipped upside down. Stepfather kicked me out of the house and you're my only friend in the world." The goat turned with the girl still clinging to its shaggy coat and lay down on a bed of fresh straw. Another goat nuzzled the girl's elbow, then another. Exhausted, Sophie snuggled up to Brutus's warm back, and the rest of the herd gathered close around. She wrapped her shawl around herself, burrowed into the hay a little and was asleep within moments.

Outside, it started to snow.

Chapter Seven
The Gingerbread House

*T*he celebration lasted several hours longer as throngs of well-wishers passed by expressing their congratulations. All too soon the event was over. Alphonse had reserved a table at a nearby tea house and the six made their way toward an open exit. A cold wind entered the building. The weather had taken an expected turn; the temperature had dropped drastically and the gentle rain that started falling at the beginning of the ceremony had turned to moderate snowfall. As the hour was getting late, Francisco and Mirna had decided that Andrew, Crestina and Ren would return home with Penn and his mounted men in the waiting carriage so as not to cause Andrew to take a chill or miss his bedtime. Bidding adieu to the trio, the issue of accommodations arose. After a quick conference, the two couples decided to continue to Francisco and Mirna's home later in the evening and retrieve Alphonse and Chantal's baggage from the Inn the next day.

In a gallant gesture, Alphonse and Francisco removed their heavier, warmer cloaks and placed them about their wives' shoulders over their lighter, fashionable wraps. The four hurried down the cobblestone streets and as they neared the nearby tea house the snowfall increased, with large, heavy flakes falling. Soon the ground was white with their rapid accumulation.

"Splendid. I love an early snowfall. I know it may warm up again for a month or so, but I always look forward to this time of year. It won't be long before the Torries are in bloom," observed Alphonse as they followed Chantal and Mirna.

Francisco said, "Yes, perfect timing for the Festival and the tribute to our wives, don't you think? Alphonse, Mirna and I were wondering if you and Chantal don't have pressing plans and if the Royal Confectionery could spare such an important man, would you two would like to stay for several weeks or perhaps through the winter? The Torries should be *muy bonita* very pretty at the 'Angel School' this year. We would enjoy your company, my friend. Certainly Andrew would." Francisco's voice trailed off.

After a moment's consideration, Alphonse responded, "Outstanding idea, Francisco. The Assistant Chief Inspector will fill in nicely. I can send him a communique. Let me approach Chantal with the idea. I cannot say for sure, but I think she would be most receptive."

Chantal's voice came over her shoulder, "Yes, I would, my darling. Mirna just asked me the same thing. I'd love to stay." And with that, the friends started making plans for the season.

"How are the other children in the Angel School?" Alphonse asked Francisco. The four turned the corner and headed towards the three-step stairway of *The Gingerbread House*, a quaint inn which served exotic teas, liqueurs, wines, pastries and delicacies from foreign lands. Due to the wide variety of its wares and its excellent cuisine, the shop enjoyed a large clientele from many nations.

Chantal and Mirna had greeted some friends and had gone ahead into the tea house.

"Much the same, my friend," sighed Francisco. He slowed, and then stopped, as did Alphonse. They stood there for a long moment. Alphonse looked down the street back towards the Great Hall. Thick, puffy snowflakes rapidly accumulated on their hair and clothing.

"Alphonse, another child has died of the ancient sickness and I could use your strength and friendship. You always seem to draw from your vast wisdom, even when you were new to the Royal Confectionary. I always appreciated that. We brought Andrew home so he may spend time with us, Alphonse. The sickness may recur soon and we want him to be with us as much as possible before that time. And, he's started coughing. But he wants to go back to school. Can you imagine that? He may be dying and he wants to be among his friends."

Alphonse nodded. "Yes. He's growing up, Francisco. It's his life. Let him go be among his friends."

Francisco said, "Thank you and yes, that is true, Alphonse, but letting go is so difficult to do." He shook his head, "The children's conditions sadden me. Just between us, I believe *adults* should be the ones to have tragedy, illness and woes befall them, not children. At least adults have had an opportunity to experience life's wonders and all that the world offers. Childhood should be an innocent, healthy and cheerful time of running with the wind on a sunny day and exploring the world. Of climbing trees and jumping into mud puddles. Not to be in pain or confined to a body that does not work. Not to be in their condition. That this happens is quite frustrating and *dios mio,* sometimes I doubt His benevolence."

Francisco paused and Alphonse noticed his friend's eyes were moistening.

He continued. "I mean, Alphonse, I know God loves us all but sometimes I simply do not understand."

The older man paused, took a deep breath, then said, "Yet, *amigo*, the children of the Angel School are often quite happy and content. Even the orphans. Do you believe it? How is this? Happy. Even the children who are worse off than Andrew. *Certainamente*, they have their bad days, but somehow I always leave happier than when I arrived. *Me*. Should it not be the other way around? I don't understand, but they have a good influence on *me*."

He stopped, and halfheartedly kicked at a drift. "I feel guilty for grumbling. I love my son and want him to experience life as I have. I want that for *all* the children. A healthy childhood. Healthy bodies for children and as adults they can get sick, that's okay with me then. Is that too much to ask?"

Alphonse started to reply but thought better and remained silent.

Francisco continued in a quiet but anguished voice, "Normal, *vato*. Is that really too much to ask for my son? Normal? Alphonse, some of the doctors want to bloodlet Andrew and other children. They say the children have too much 'humor'. Both Mirna and I think the idea is foolish beyond the imagination. Some less civilized nations put these children to death. Can you imagine that? These children have done nothing wrong. Praise God our beautiful Tierary will not permit such barbarism. I know he has but a year or so before he truly will grow sick even if his cough is nothing. I am starting to get desperate for my son."

He stopped, put a hand up to his face and in a hoarse voice croaked, "It's so hard staying strong for Mirna and Andrew. I cannot bear it alone."

A sudden commotion on the other side of the street broke Francisco's angst and brought their right hands to the hilts of their swords and their left hands to draw their pistols. Alphonse instinctively whirled and checked behind for marauders who might have used the disruption across the street to attack from the rear, but it was just a pair of bawdy couples passing by, throwing snow at each other, their loud, drunken laughter interrupting the moment. The men looked at each other. Francisco clucked his tongue. "My how the training comes back after all these years, my friend."

Alphonse smiled. " 'Training becomes the man; the man becomes the training.' Chief Petty Officer Rochileau used to say that when he was preparing his wet-behind-the-ears seadogs to be officers, and he's right once again."

The men holstered their pistols. Alphonse continued, "Francisco, we must remember that the Lord has made even the most gnarled of trees lovely in their own way. And he has done so with the children. I don't know why or how the children are as they are, but I know their happiness reflects His glory. All creation declares God's majesty. And recall that in Heaven there is no pain, no paralysis. Certainly no suffering. Focus on that, Francisco. Tell the children about the Lord always. Because their future can be so large but their present is so small."

He cleared his throat and repeated, "So very small." Alphonse wavered. "And, Andrew's cough can be from many reasons, Francisco, not just the final sickness. Are there no herbs, poultices, or tinctures to treat it? Surely Chantal and Mirna can concoct some potion to give him."

Francisco started to shake his head but stopped, his eyebrows arched with hope. "No *amigo*, nothing yet." He snapped his fingers. "You know what? I have noticed when Andrew is in the underground passageway he seems to have more energy and seems healthier. Perhaps that should be explored. Yes indeed, I shall mention this to them. This is an excellent thought."

Francisco and Alphonse paused near the entrance for a moment, under a snow laden elm tree. Francisco turned and gripped his friend's shoulder. "You are a good man, Alphonse. Thank you for putting that back into perspective. Sometimes when man doubts God's wisdom we forget that God is in control, not man." Francisco raised his eyes to the Heavens and said in a quiet voice, "I'm sorry, Lord." He turned and his scabbard smacked the trunk of the tree, causing a bit of accumulation from an overloaded branch to slip off its perch and land on his head.

Sputtering, he brushed it off and observed, "Proof positive God has a sense of humor, *amigo*."

Alphonse laughed as he and Francisco moved to rejoin the ladies. Francisco quickly regained his composure and continued, "So, we have plans to visit the Angel School in a few days. We shall be able to visit the staff and Nonna Maria. Perhaps some of the children, too. Praise God for Nonna Maria, the headmistress of the school. I do not know what we would do without her. She has a big heart for the little ones. Nonna Maria is quite fond of you and Chantal. She will be there when we stop by. Nonna always is."

The men continued into the tea house and followed the waiter as he showed them where the ladies were already seated at a comfortable table close to the hearth. Soon the four had shaken off the chill and ordered their meals.

Conversation again turned to Andrew. "It was good for me to see Andrew so happy," said Alphonse. "He deserves many more days of happiness like this one."

Francisco replied, "Yes he does. Alphonse, you should have seen how excited he was when I told him two weeks ago about the tribute for tonight. Andrew was almost beside himself. He could hardly sleep for days. Never have I seen him so. Of one thing I am certain – our little Andrew can keep a big secret."

8
Chapter Eight
Penn

*A*ndrew spent weekdays at the *Le Ballet avec des Anges* Special Boarding School for Children, but unlike most of the children, came home each weekend. Penn the Scot, Chief of the Stables and Captain of the Carriage at *La Estancia*, told anyone in earshot that transporting Andrew to and from school was his personal duty and special privilege. Although muscular and huge in stature, Penn was gentle and a man of few words. In fact, the townspeople often said that his kindly heart was bigger than his body, if that were possible. Many years ago, while in military service to His Majesty in the Royal Calvary, during the far away war, the Scot had been knocked off his steed and captured in the mountains by the enemy. Penn had returned to a hero's welcome at the end of the war and was decorated for gallantry and bravery by the king.

Unfortunately, like many veterans, the Scot carried painful memories of combat and the grim treatment received at the hands of his captors. Because of an unsuccessful escape attempt with five other prisoners, Penn had been beaten and tortured, then confined for two years in a wooden box not quite large enough to stand in. Three of his fellow escapees were captured and likewise confined. Another had lost an arm in the endeavor and only the careful ministrations of his fellow prisoners saved his life. The fifth escapee was beheaded as an example to the others. Yet despite savage beatings administered by the guards, Penn and his fellow confinees yelled encouragement across the grounds to each other and in time became close friends despite the distance.

Upon his release and return to Tierary, whenever Penn would attempt to talk about his wartime experiences, his gruff voice would start out strong and forceful then gradually falter as his words became choked by the tremendous emotions underneath.

At the urging of family and friends, Penn would endeavor to continue but soon the Scot's words would soon trail off and stop; he would stare off into the distance, either unable or unwilling to vocalize his pain. The gentle giant adopted the policy of never speaking about the war with anyone except his former comrades-in-arms, and then only rarely.

But sometimes deep into the night, the Scot's inner turmoil would boil over and his unconscious thrashing about would awaken Giselle, his wife, who would hold him in her arms and pray, wiping away both her tears and his as her husband again relived the war's horror in his dreams.

During his captivity, the stout wooden cell that defined Penn's world had narrow slit openings on the sides and door. A single ventilation hole in the top allowed him to see the blue sky and some overhanging trees. Unknown to his captors, Penn had enlarged the hole from the inside by pulling splinters away from the opening with his fingernails just enough to press his nose through and smell the wind rushing down from the hills and mountains around the prison camp. The fast moving currents of air would sometimes carry familiar scents, which prompted fond memories of fast, unfettered rides on the moors and highlands of his home.

Penn and his fellow prisoners hated "the box" and in a perverse gesture of defiance, nicknamed themselves the "Innies" while referring to the other prisoners as "Outies." In the early months of their confinement, the Innies determined not to let their captors extend the physical confinement to their minds as well.

Each day from noon until evening as the rest of the prisoners were being fed and exercised and the noise level in prisoner of war camp was highest, the Innies would call to each other in Scottish Gaelic, the ancient language of Scotland that Penn had taught the Innies and several other warriors in the months before their capture. He and his fellow Innies would participate in verbal exercises whereby the three would pretend that they were riding their steeds in echelon attack formation, descending down from high in the hills above on their victims, launching bold, successful strikes on enemy targets. The exercise lasted until the evening meal.

For hours after the operation was over the Outies would covertly toss small-well aimed rocks at the men's boxes; each soft *thwack* on the outside of the box signifying that the three men were loved and not forgotten by their fellows on the outside. After two years of confinement, the prison camp officials decided that the Innies had been punished enough and ordered them beaten and released. At the end of the war Penn and the Innies had each brought home a small rock from outside their box; these now hung on leather thongs around their necks.

The years of imprisonment had instilled in Penn a strong sense of the preciousness of freedom. The Scot saw that Andrew also loved the raw feeling of the wind as it swept across his face, and recognized the boy as a kindred spirit.

The veteran then determined he would provide the boy with what he thought was the truest sense of freedom. With Francisco's tacit approval, each Monday morning and Friday afternoon the gentle giant would gather the youth into his massive arms and would climb up to the driver's seat of *Corsair*, his personal carriage.

With a light but secure grip on his charge, Penn would cradle Andrew on his lap and declare in his thick Scottish brogue, "Aye, laddie, we've much in common, now, haven't we? What kind of bird do ye want to be today? A falcon? Perhaps an eagle, then? What's that yer sayin' man? Can ye be both? *Both*? Well now, aye, of course, laddie. The courage of an eagle defending his land; the agility of a falcon preparing to strike? Aye, I see yer wisdom, a fine choice indeed. Let us fly as an eagle-falcon this day."

His voice rising with excitement, Penn would continue, "Ready? Andrew, me lad, do ya have yer brass horn, man? Good. Let's be free, then, FREE, *FREE*, FREE."

With a loud roar and a tremendous crack of his whip, Penn would send the horse and carriage flying at breakneck speed careening down the country lanes with Andrew laughing and honking his horn with glee to warn unsuspecting folks ahead.

Chapter Nine
The Two Princes

A sudden influx of hungry festival attendees had oc-cupied the empty tables and booths of the Ginger-bread House. The headwaiter stopped by and served a steaming pot of Oolong tea and an exquisite platter of con-fectioneries. "Compliments of that chap right over there." The waiter pointed in the direction of a well-dressed gentleman seated at the rear of the shop.

A wide smile creased his ebony face as the Prime Direc-tor of the United Confectionery House in Deltanos tipped his brimmed hat in salute. "Prince Solomon. A finer gentleman simply cannot be found," exclaimed Alphonse, who rose to his feet and strode over to greet his friend. With genuine affec-tion, the two bear hugged, chatted for several moments, then turned and approached the table. "Prince Solomon. How mar-velous to see you again. How are things in your great country of Deltanos?"

Alphonse introduced Chantal and Mirna, who thanked the prince for his thoughtfulness.

Prince Solomon, charming as always, kissed the ladies' ex-tended hands. "You're most welcome. I finally get to meet the Mothers of the Torrie Rose. Seldom has such beauty existed in one place. I have heard so much about you, Chantal and you,

Mirna, but I must protest that your husbands' words did not do either of you justice," said the prince in a lilting accent that reminded one of exotic lands.

Flattered, the ladies laughed and the prince continued, "But much to their credit, no words could. And, dear ladies, it is with great pleasure that I make your acquaintance. I congratulate you on your tribute this evening. Your achievement and the display were marvelous."

Francisco rose and bowed with respect, then smiled and gave his own bear hug to the man. "Prince Solomon, how good to see you, my friend. How long has it been?"

Prince Solomon laughed, "Too long, Francisco, much too long. There is opportunity aplenty for those with vision and grit, both in Tierary and Deltanos these days. We have much to discuss. Pardon me for not staying longer, but my time here in the Gingerbread House is limited, as is the time left in my confectionery house. *Charcané*, my estate in southern Deltanos, summons me."

Alphonse and Francisco exchanged glances and smiled.

Prince Solomon continued, "I must be on my way, yet I have a rather odd request. Could we five perhaps meet at your estate tomorrow in the early afternoon for a brief appointment? There are important matters to discuss with the former and present Chief Divinity Inspectors and indeed, the Mothers of the Torrie Rose, as well."

The friends looked at each other and nodded in assent. Francisco responded, "Of course, Solomon. A late lunch, perhaps, my friend? Or an early dinner?"

The prince nodded. "Either would be fine."

Francisco smiled, "Then we shall see you early in the afternoon. Now, my good friend, it is a far carriage ride to *La Estancia* and the roads are not always safe after twilight. Please consider staying over the night as well. You and your staff are always welcome in our home." He smiled, "And would you care to join us now on this special evening?"

The prince laughed, bowed, and flashed his handsome smile. "Unfortunately, I cannot, as I must tend to some pressing matters." He paused, threw back his head and laughed, revealing white, straight, even teeth. "But your hospitality is renowned the world over, Francisco. I have fond recollections of my stay in *La Estancia* several years ago. In fact, I believe your son Andrew was just a few years old then and your lovely wife was away at Alphonse's estate visiting Chantal. Come to think about it, yes, I shall accept your gracious invitation. I should very much like to stay over the night. Although my staff shall remain at the Inn, I shall bring my young protégé." He leaned in as if to share a secret. "I trust you to keep this confidential; unlike me, Prince Samuel is in line for the throne someday. Samuel is traveling with the circus in order to know our citizens and those of the lands he will deal with when he someday rules our country. He is a smart, talented and funny man, and bills himself as the "Prince of Clowns". Well, I must be on my way, then. Enjoy the platter and we shall see you tomorrow in the early afternoon. Pleasant evening, then."

Prince Solomon bowed, tipped his fedora and made his way past the other tables and out the door.

Alphonse wondered out loud, "While Solomon seems to be of good cheer, I detected a bit of tension in his voice. I wonder what's going on and why he wants to visit tomorrow."

Chantal said, "I cannot venture to guess what Prince Solomon would like to see *us* for, Mirna. I rather think that perhaps he just likes our cuisine." The four grinned and just then their orders arrived.

The music was exquisite. Sophie and the lad from the carriage were dancing all by themselves amidst dozens of couples in a magnificent ballroom. As he twirled her about, servants and guests stood at the sides of the dance floor, applauding their graceful moves. The music softened for a moment, the light dimmed, and he presented her with a soft red rose. The rose changed color, first to cinnamon then orange and then to burgundy. Delighted, she reached for the blossom, but somehow it turned into a soft white goose feather, which he teasingly ran over her face, chin and lips, lightly. And again. She laughed, her heart bursting with joy. Suddenly a most obnoxious odor filled the room. The music faded, the servants turned away, and the boy pulled back, somehow becoming fuzzy and distant. She felt the feather's touch again, this time starting under her chin and then tickling her nostrils. Annoyed, Sophie pushed it away – and awoke to find a flatulent stray feline lying on her chest, its tail flicking over her face. "Cats can be so irritating," she thought as she shooed it away, rolled over and drifted back to sleep.

Alas, the boy was gone.

Chapter Ten
La Estancia

"*Bastante.* Enough. What a tasty meal," announced Francisco. "I am truly unable to eat another bite." He pushed back his chair to give himself more room.

Alphonse questioned, "I say, old chap, not even if the Royal Confectionery has chosen this time to unveil their newest confection?"

Francisco quickly pushed his chair back to the table. "You have my complete attention, *amigo,*" he said.

Alphonse and the ladies smiled as Alphonse went on, "Do you recall two years ago sending me an idea for a certain confectionery made of chocolate, custard and coconut? I believe you called it a 'Custard Ball Meltover'."

Francisco's faraway look prompted the Chief Divinity Inspector to hesitate for a moment and clear his throat. "Harrumph. Yes, well, at any rate, I forwarded the recipe to our culinary artists to create, but somehow, *amigo,* your ingenuity was received but never developed. One day about a year ago, during cleaning, a clerk found your recipe behind some storage crates. From what I could tell, the wind had blown the paper off his desk and had come to rest there. He came by my office, apologized and asked me if we should proceed with your idea. I was quite busy at the time and answered "of course" but

I must confess that I lost track of development until a week ago. I say, sorry, old chap. As former Chief Divinity Inspector, you know that there is about a one year lag from concept to the actual creation."

Alphonse paused again as if to collect his thoughts, and then with a sheepish look on his face continued, "Right, old man. I was never any good at this sort of formality."

The Chief Divinity Inspector took a small golden box from his traveling bag and placed it on the table in front of Francisco. "From Snorffleham Palace and the king himself. But somehow, this divinity is addressed to Andrew."

Francisco sat still for a moment, and then with a wide smile, slid the box in front of Mirna. "Our Sing Song Child has been honored by the king. This *has* been quite a memorable evening."

Alphonse looked at Francisco for clarification, who grinned and said, "There is a story behind this, *amigo*. We shall tell you tomorrow in the morning. With Andrew present of course."

Mirna gave her husband a gentle kiss and put the golden box into her purse.

After a moment, Chantal said brightly, "Shall we be on our way then?"

Francisco motioned to the waiter and called out, "*La cuenta, por favor, señor.* The check, please. And, if you would, call our warm carriage and our contingent of armed escorts to take us home."

Ten minutes later, a slick black carriage with the name *Thunderchief* painted in fancy scroll work on the door under the driver and pulled by four spirited black horses, drew up to the curb outside the bistro. The carriage was driven by a fellow prisoner-of-war comrade of Penn's, a ruddy-faced Innie named Peel. Six armed and mounted men waited nearby, for the hills and roads were home to lawless bands of thieves and attackers.

The snowfall had slowed and over three inches had accumulated on the ground.

As Alphonse stepped off the curb, he slipped on an icy patch on the cobblestones and fell forward, sharply banging his forehead on the side of the coach and stepping with both feet into an ankle-deep slush-filled puddle. For a moment his vision fogged and he saw an angel sitting on the roof of the carriage. He was shocked when the angel smiled and waved at him, then disappeared. Peel grabbed Alphonse by the arm to steady him. The misstep into the water soaked through his fancy boots to his stockings. Although quite groggy, Alphonse shook off the water, thanked his driver and alerted the others to the hazard.

The carriage was pulled forward and another misstep was avoided.

Francisco gave directions to the driver as the ladies climbed into the carriage. Chantal came to her woozy husband's rescue, cradling his head in her lap. She insisted on stopping at a deeper snowy patch of ground so she could gather some snow into her scarf for a makeshift cold pack for the large bump emerging on his forehead.

Under her careful ministrations, Alphonse soon felt better and sat up the remainder of the journey. The trip to *La Estancia*, usually long and arduous, was quick and soon the tired but contented couples were standing in the foyer of the main house.

Mirna spoke up, "As Prince Solomon and Prince Samuel will be staying in the guest house tomorrow night. Knowing my generous husband, he will insist that they stay for several days longer."

Alphonse rose to his friend's defense. "But my dear Mirna, he has a reputation to protect."

Mirna continued, "That is true. Until they depart, would you mind staying in the first guest chambers next to Andrew? You can move to the guest house when the princes leave."

Chantal spoke for the two. "Certainly, Mirna. After all, how often do you have the opportunity to entertain royalty?"

Alphonse said, "Before we turn in, let us share one last cup of tea – chamomile this time – and a sampling of the Royal Confectionery's finest truffles. I still have a headache but altogether, my head feels better thanks to my wife's gentle care. On this special day with you, our dear friends, we should linger until the small hours of the morning; however not in an unpleasant fashion. I simply must change from my soggy socks and shoes into warm and dry footwear."

Mirna and Chantal headed toward the kitchen.

After a moment's reflection, Francisco said, "There are slippers in your chambers, my friend. And a sampling of dark chocolate, lemon, raspberry and coconut truffles would be well received."

Alphonse grinned, "I have a small sampling of Truffoons, Francisco. Newest product line from the firm. Everything else is in our quarters in the Whittleford Inn."

Francisco laughed and said, "Truffoons? Truffles and what? Ah, a compilation. I knew I left the Royal Confectionery in good hands. On your way then, *amigo. Vamanos.* Let's go. We shall see you in the kitchen. And bring them all."

Alphonse grinned, picked up a candle for illumination and started up the stairs. As he reached the top of the staircase, faint strains of a beautiful melody reached his ears.

Alphonse paused, turned the corner, and moved down the hallway towards the source of the sound. The music grew louder and lovelier. Turning yet another corner, to his utter amazement, he saw a bright, warm, golden light shining from Andrew's partly open chamber door illuminating the wooden floor and wall opposite the doorway.

As he shuffled toward the light and music, Alphonse saw shadows of dancing figures on the far wall. He squinted into the room and for the briefest of moments, just as his eyes were adjusting to the bright light, Alphonse was startled to see what appeared to be a smiling Andrew holding Ren the cat, dancing and singing in harmony with other youths from the Angel School. Suddenly, the light and music winked out, replaced by the normal shadows and sounds of the night. Andrew lay asleep on his bed, wheeled-chair parked in the corner. His breathing was deep and even; the boy was gently snoring. Ren was curled up on Andrew's chest and twitching as if chasing a mouse.

"I say, that couldn't have happened," Alphonse said aloud in a quavery voice. "No. Certainly not. Quite impossible." Yet the music seemed somehow familiar. The Chief Divinity Inspector's brow furrowed as he tried to recall where he had heard the melody before, but to no avail.

When he returned to the kitchen, Alphonse queried Chantal, Francisco and Mirna about the incident. The three said that they had not heard any music or seen any light, but he had the feeling that perhaps something was being left unsaid by his friends. Alphonse tried to push the occurrence from his mind and enjoy the rest of the evening. The truffoons were an instant hit; dark chocolate truffles with slivers of caramel and macaroon cookie a welcome treat, and at last the couples decided to retire.

A gentle rat-a-tat-tat sound on the door ushered in an early start of the new day.

Alphonse awoke, yawned, put on his robe and slipped on his borrowed slippers. He grumbled, "Good grief, the sun is not even up yet," but good-naturedly padded over to the door. Much to his surprise, Teresa, the diminutive cook, stood in the hallway with a large, covered silver tray in her hands and an even larger smile on her weathered face.

"*Buenos días Señor* Alphonse. Welcome again to *La Estancia*. How is your head? It looks pretty good. So, I have breakfast for you and *La Señora Chantal. Desayuno* the way you like it: *huevos rancheros, guacamole, corn tortillas y salsa picanté.* But I remember from the last visit you like tea and not *café.*"

Chantal stirred in bed and called out, "Who is there, darling?"

Alphonse took the tray, turned and smiled. "*Señora* Teresa with breakfast." Turning back to Teresa, Alphonse continued, "Teresa. Wonderful to see you again as well. My head feels better. Thank you for your concern. Good news. We're staying the winter, so if you could, would you please teach me your recipe for that splendid *carne asada* that you made when we were last here?"

Teresa replied, "Staying the winter? *Magnifico. Señor* Alphonso, I shall teach you how to cook carne asada and much more."

She paused, peered up her nose through her spectacles and waggled her finger at Alphonse. "But I must be truthful. *Su esposa, La Señora* Chantal, is a much more skillful cook than you."

A snort, then muffled giggles came from the direction of *La Señora* Chantal.

Teresa grinned. "But for now I must go. *Doña* Mirna is busy in the kitchen and I have much work to do."

Alphonse paused and said in a lower voice, "Teresa, may I ask you a question? Are you aware of something, well, perhaps a bit odd about Andrew's quarters at night?"

Teresa's brows furrowed in concentration as she searched her memory. Finally, she brightened. "No, *Señor* Alphonso, nothing odd. I just know it is the room of a happy *niño*. And now the room of a happy *gato* too."

A perplexed look on his face, Alphonse thanked Teresa again for making breakfast and closed the door with his elbow. Still holding the tray in front of him, he leaned back against the door and mumbled, "Indeed. The scene seemed so real to me. The light. Andrew dancing. And that music. I just know that I've heard that melody somewhere before."

Chantal arose from the bed and put on her robe and slippers. She walked over to where Alphonse was holding the tray and examined his head with care. Satisfied, she planted a tender kiss on his forehead, turned, and removed the covers on each dish.

She said, "Yes, your head seems much better than last night. Yum. And I do so love Teresa's breakfasts." Chantal took the provided silverware, place mats, and tea setting, and set the table in the alcove in front of the window.

When she was seated, Chantal poured tea for two and remarked, "Come to *desayuno*, my love, but don't forget to bring the tray. And perhaps I shall make Teresa's carne asada for you someday."

Alphonse set the tray on the table. "Harrumph. Perhaps I shall surprise *you* one day with my culinary skills, *La Señora* Chantal." Changing the direction of the conversation, he continued, "After breakfast, let us keep our custom of reading the bible and praying as one."

Chantal replied, "Alphonse, your leadership blesses me. Let us now thank God for what He has provided." The two held hands and bowed their heads as Alphonse asked the Lord to bless the meal, their marriage, and the days ahead.

A dull pain burned through her side, waking Sophie. She shifted her body away from the discomfort, which subsided, but was replaced by a hard and unyielding pressure against her hip. Sleepily, she remembered the shard of pottery and the clay disk she had found the afternoon before, and took out both pieces from her pocket. Her weight had pressed the earthenware shard's edge at an angle against the disk and in the dimness Sophie could see a bit of clay had broken off. There seemed to be something inside; something round, flat and hard. With her fingernail Sophie started picking at the clay, revealing a glint of metal. More picking and a gob of spit liberally applied revealed a silver coin, enough money to feed her family for a month. Stepfather could buy another ox or even enough lumber to add a room to their home. Another dab of spit rubbed and cleaned up the coin enough to see some words in a strange language and the head of a man, the same man with the funny nose on the shard of pottery.

Rising excitement in her heart was tempered by her surroundings. No, she was now a child without a family, soon to be a homeless urchin. Stepfather had kicked her out last night. She was alone, abandoned.

She started to cry, then forced herself to stop. Self-pity wouldn't help matters now, and at least she wouldn't have to hide from *him* anymore.

The goats started to rustle with the coming dawn, and she knew she had to plan her next moves carefully. Sophie knelt on the straw, scrunched her eyes tightly and quietly asked God for direction, protection and an angel to guide her. Yes, Lord, please send an angel, she thought. Then it hit her. That's the answer: an angel. Sophie wrapped her shawl, took down a milking bowl from the wall and quickly milked Mia, her favorite nannie goat. She drank her fill, then more. From the family larder she took a thick wedge of cheese, ate a large bite then drank more milk. Next, she took down a warm but smelly blanket from a nail, wrapped a sheaf of straw securely around her legs and feet then quietly opened the barn door.

Almost three inches of snow had fallen during the night and, with a shudder, she stepped out into the cold whiteness. She was shocked to see large footprints on the path leading from the house to the barn, marks that abruptly stopped halfway and turned back to the house. Now even more determined to leave, she headed for the *Le Ballet avec des Anges*, Special Boarding School for Children, for some reason known to the populace as the "Angel School".

Outside the window the sun was declaring its intentions to rise. Alphonse, Francisco and Andrew had sequestered themselves in the drawing room for a few hours and immersed themselves in setting up their new venture. The three had done this many times over the past year.

They had put their heads together and had defined several problem areas associated with the transport of perishable foodstuffs. Alphonse and Francisco had developed solutions to these problems and had decided to start their own company.

Despite his young age, Andrew seemed to grasp the idea of a company-on-paper and listened intently as he had so many times before.

At last the men were satisfied with their efforts. They gathered the plans into a waterproof leather brief, bound it with a leather strap, and made their way toward the front gate.

A short while later, a trio of riders trotted up to the front gate, received a package from the waiting Alphonse and Francisco and galloped away.

Mirna and Chantal had left *La Estancia* with Penn on *Corsair* the carriage for a speedy journey into town. The ladies were to retrieve Chantal and Alphonse's belongings from the Inn. On their way back they were to stop at the Whittleford open air marketplace to purchase the choicest foodstuffs for the impending royal visit.

Chapter Eleven
Announcements

Mirna and Chantal walked through the marketplace gates and noticed a large group of townspeople gathered in the center of the courtyard.

As they neared, they saw the crowd watching a tall man with curly orange hair and a long white wispy beard, dressed in a bright crimson robe and cobalt blue conical hat. With exaggerated clumsy and bumbling efforts, the figure had overturned a large, head-high empty wooden crate and was now trying to climb upon the top. His efforts were comical, almost buffoon-like. Several of the townspeople started to snicker, and then many started openly laughing at his efforts. A man in the back of the crowd yelled "Jester" and the audience cheered. Attached to his right hand was a long white cord tied to a large, flat, multicolored silken bag. The cord hindered the man's movements and soon had looped itself around his outstretched arms and legs. As a fly's struggle for freedom from a spider's web serves only to further ensnare, the man had become so tangled in the cord that he could not move. Standing straight upright, he stood still; the figure then lowered his arms to his waist and shrugged his shoulders thrice. To the amazement of the crowd, the cord leaped off his body and landed in a heap on the ground. The odd fellow then resumed his efforts to climb the crate. There. He was up.

To the sound of applause, the man lay on his stomach with his eyes closed, his panting audible to the crowd for several seconds. He gathered his strength, then stood upright in one quick motion He looped the long white cord in a pile at his feet, then hauled the silken bag up to the top of the crate.

As if for the first time he noticed the crowd. A tiny smile grew, and then blossomed into a huge grin on his white painted face. The smile, framed by a large berry-red oval surrounding his lips, appeared odd yet appropriate considering his oversized, bulbous aqua nose and large bright green ovals painted from his eyes up to his forehead.

A group of small children toward the front of the crowd waved their hands at the man. He waved back with both white-mittened hands, and then started jumping up and down in an enthusiastic response.

Oh no! The white cord somehow wrapped itself around his legs and the odd fellow tripped and lost his balance.

The crowd gasped as the man, arms wind-milling, swayed first to the left, regained his equilibrium, over corrected, then swayed back to the right and finally back to the left again. At each time the performer seemed to regain his balance at the last moment before falling off in a remarkable display of body control.

The crowd oohed and aahed at his efforts, their nervous laughter growing with each motion, and applauding his success when he slowed and came to a stop in the middle of the crate. He took a little bow for the crowd, who reacted with even more enthusiastic cheering and clapping. Pleased by their response, he took an even larger bow, much to the delight of the throng. He then bent over from the waist as if to take a gigantic bow but stopped with his head down and rummaged about in his multicolored silk bag; emerging with a large, bright, hand painted sign which he lifted with triumph into the air with both hands.

Cheers, laughter, and a current of excitement ran through the crowd.

The circus. The circus was coming to town.

Not just any old big-top but the Banouso and Wisbar Greater-than-Great World Famous Family Circus from Deltanos. The man then jumped down from the crate and started passing out handbills to the eager and receptive crowd. About that time, other men attired in similar outlandish garb appeared and tacked signs with the same information on lamp posts throughout the city.

The signs proclaimed three performances one week from today on Babak's farm in the outskirts of Whittleford. Townspeople young and old were invited and children were to be admitted at half price. What's more, there were to be free potatoes for all.

Another sign announced a circus parade through downtown in six days. The parade was to be just before midday; the sign also urged people to buy tickets for the performances at the local weaver's shop.

The weaver, a tall, lanky, easy going Englishman named Ayres, was offering a substantial discount to children and veterans of the Far Away War. Like Penn and Peel, Ayres had also been knocked off his steed, captured and held by the enemy in the same prison. Upon their release, the grateful king had recognized the three – and many others – as heroes. Like his fellow former prisoners, Ayres kept a speedy carriage for hire and had named it *Phantom*.

Mirna and Chantal hurried through the marketplace, their practiced eyes and hands making quick decisions on the quality of vegetables, fruit, and foodstuffs to be purchased.

The ladies concluded their transactions and headed back to the rendezvous point where Penn would pick them up. The three were to swing by the Inn to pick up Chantal and Alphonse's baggage.

As the women climbed into the carriage at the Inn, Chantal had a sudden inspiration and turning to Mirna, said, "Perhaps we could purchase enough circus tickets to take Andrew and all the children from the Angel School." She looked toward the back of the carriage. Penn was still busy loading baggage in the aft compartment. As he completed his task, he climbed up onto his perch and soon the carriage was off, trailed as always by an armed entourage.

"It would be greatly beneficial for them," said Mirna as the carriage bounced along. She paused as if considering a thought, then continued, "Great idea, Chantal. But instead of us buying tickets, do you think the local businesses would buy them to donate to the school? Say, maybe the Bottington-Downs Wax Figurine and Candle Company should have the Mothers of the Torrie Rose pay them a visit. They could make a beautiful, glowing donation."

"Capital idea, Mirna," Chantal snickered. "And let us not forget our connections with the Royal Confectionery. I am sure our husbands could persuade them to make a sweet and tasty contribution."

The ladies started laughing with their silliness. Chantal continued, "Say, maybe all the peddlers in town could use such a visit. The paper and twine merchants could wrap up the bargain. Then we could use glue from the tannery to seal the deal."

Ooof. The wagon hit a bump, sending the ladies airborne for a moment.

The ladies were laughing even harder when Mirna added, "The suspender and belt makers could hold up their end." By this time the ladies were laughing so hard that they were rolling on the seats, gasping for breath.

Penn turned from his perch and contributed, "Ay, pardon the intrusion, lassies, but me second cousins Archibald and Macleod's blacksmithery forges hammers and nails that could help drive the point home." The three laughed even harder as Chantal said, "Yes, but the tobacconist shop might go up in smoke." Their hilarity continued and the sounds of merriment far preceded the carriage.

Humor and a speedy set of horses had made the long drive seem short as the trio arrived at *La Estancia*. Alphonse and Francisco greeted their wives as they entered the kitchen through the rear entrance. The men had joined Andrew and Crestina for the almost-midday repast.

The ladies gathered around the seated figures and in a covert motion, Mirna showed the box to Francisco.

Francisco nodded and cleared his throat. "Ahhhem, Andrew, we have two things *muy importante*, very important to discuss."

Mirna interrupted, "Guess what, Andrew. The circus is coming to town and there is to be a parade in six days."

The announcement brought a shine to the boy's eyes.

Mother and son hugged, and Andrew queried, "Iillere e iegrs en onkies? En I ide am ephant?"

Although the words came with difficulty, there was no mistaking the excitement in his voice.

With a twinkle in her eyes, Mirna replied, "Tigers and monkeys? Of course, silly; it's a circus. But to ride an elephant is dangerous, *mijo*. Do you think you're up to the task?"

Andrew's lopsided smile grew. He threw out his chest and said, "Oh es, Omma. I an anle e east. I a eming a an, an Ren ill elp."

Everyone started laughing with Andrew.

Mirna continued, "Yes, I think you can handle the beast. And yes, you are becoming a man, and Ren will indeed help. Then perhaps you may get your wish, my son. Do you recall meeting Prince Solomon the last time he visited? Your father was here with you as I was visiting Chantal at the time. You were much younger then."

Andrew nodded. "Orof."

"Sort of. Yes. Good. His friend, Samuel, is one of the entertainers in the circus. Samuel calls himself the Prince of Clowns. He and Solomon will be staying with us in the guesthouse for a few days. Maybe he will show you some clown tricks. They will be arriving this afternoon." Mirna paused. "And that reminds me, young man, you must tidy up your room before their visit. We must make a good impression on the Prince of Clowns."

Andrew nodded vigorously. "Wha es e otr nouemet?"

Mirna's expression queried her husband. Francisco feigned ignorance for a moment until one of Mirna's elbows brought his memories back. He said, "Oh, yes, *Tio* Alphonse gave this to us last night. From the king. This box is for you."

Mirna handed the golden box to Francisco, who placed it on the table in front of Andrew.

Andrew grasped the box between his wrists and Francisco opened the lid, their actions revealing a smooth teamwork that had been honed over the years. "You see, Andrew, when the Royal Confectionery decides to produce a new treat, there is only a single piece made until the creator of the treat can confirm that the idea and the finished product are the same. Do you remember one night just over two years ago when we were playing confection designer in the kitchen? You mixed your special custard, coconut, and bittersweet chocolate together and we put the tin in the oven? You do? *Bueno*. Good. Well, as you recall, the concoction melted into a ball and you called it a "Custard Ball Meltover." We laughed at the idea, but I put your thoughts on paper and now the king wants to know if this is what you had intended."

Francisco took out the treat, placed the morsel on the plate in front of his son and cut it into five sections. He put a piece in Andrew's mouth.

Andrew's eyes grew wide as he savored the flavor. He smiled, "*Sí,* Apa, tis es e eal ing."

Francisco smiled and replied, "The real thing indeed. Well then, *joven,* young man, I shall alert the King that the newest designer for the Royal Confectionery has approved of his efforts. They may start production now. Congratulations, my son."

All the astonished youth managed to say was "Oh," as the five adults alternately hugged and congratulated him. The sweet moment lasted for several minutes until Teresa walked in and asked when the princes were to arrive. She was told of Andrew's honor and offered her congratulations as well.

Andrew and Crestina then headed upstairs, for the Royal Confectionery's youngest employee was determined to test his newfound strength and to make his parents proud of how he cleaned his room.

Chapter Twelve
Arrivals

The snowfall of the previous night had started to melt with the sunrise and by mid-morning the dry, thirsty ground had consumed almost every trace of moisture. Soon it was early afternoon. A refreshing cold wind came from the north, and delicate cirrus clouds high in the Heavens provided a pleasant contrast to the deep blue sky.

Andrew and Crestina were up on the roof's lookout deck. Crestina pointed up at the sky. "Mare's tails. Look, Andrew, do you see the white, wispy clouds high in the sky? They are called mare's tails. When you see them they are a sign that there is a weather change soon to come. If you ask me, there's snow on the way, with the fast way the weather changes here, perhaps even tonight, and maybe even as much as shin deep."

Andrew nodded in agreement and added, "En eh orrries ill loom oon."

He was the first to spy a solitary figure approach the front gate from his vantage point and was beside himself with joy. "Ook, Ren, ei an se Ona Ria an omon lse." The little cat yawned then licked Andrew's nose. The boy laughed and said, "Ona Ria" again and again as the figure neared.

Soon, a worn carriage pulled by an old swaybacked mare with a dusty pink and blue straw bonnet on its head clomped up the road, through the front gates and into the courtyard.

The carriage pulled up to the main entrance to the house. The driver was an older, heavyset woman wearing a loose-fitting black skirt and blouse. Over these she wore a worn black traveling cloak. Perched on her head was a straw bonnet similar to the horses'. Her slate gray hair was gathered into a bun at the back of her neck, making her hooked nose appear beaklike on her weathered, leathery face. Seated on the bench next to her and holding on tightly was a thin, exhausted looking twelve year old girl.

Servants announced Nonna Maria's arrival to Francisco and Mirna, who went outside to receive their guest.

"Nonna Maria. How are you? What a pleasant surprise." said Mirna as Francisco assisted her and her companion down from the carriage and retrieved her bag. With genuine warmth, Mirna hugged the teacher in greeting and said, "So good to see you again. What brings you to *La Estancia*? You will of course be our guest for the evening and perhaps several days with us, yes?"

Nonna Maria bowed and said, "Yes, thank you. We are exhausted, and would be honored. Mirna and Francisco, I found this young lady on the road yesterday. She had been thrown out of her home by her stepfather. She is now under my protection and will join the children of the Angel School."

Mirna turned to the girl who had molded herself to Nonna Maria's ample frame and said warmly, "And whom have we here?"

The girl shyly extended her hand and said in a tiny voice, "My name is Sophie."

"Well, Sophie, welcome to our home. You look famished. Can we get you something to eat?" The girl nodded and answered, "Yes, please. Something warm. Something hot."

Mirna smiled and summoned a house maid. "This is a godly home, Sophie. Whatever has happened to you before will not happen any longer. You are safe here, and you always will be welcome. Go with the maid and she will see to it you get a bath and clean clothes. When you are dressed, please come and join us for something to eat."

Just then Alphonse, Chantal and Teresa arrived. Francisco ushered the group into the receiving room of the main house. In their haste to welcome Nonna Maria and Sophie, the servants had left the front door open.

Alphonse moved to close the door. In the excitement, Teresa and Mirna had hurried off toward the kitchen to prepare tea and some food for Sophie. Halfway there, Teresa shooed Mirna back into the receiving room, saying that the Doña Mirna was the Lady of the House, and must go to be with Nonna Maria. Besides, she, Teresa, would be faster preparing the refreshments herself and would personally oversee Sophie's care.

Mirna hugged Teresa then turned and went to rejoin the others.

Nonna Maria took off her cloak and bonnet. Chantal reached for them only to be relieved of the garments by Francisco, who hung them on one of the gilded pegs in the coat closet.

Chantal made sure Nonna Maria was comfortable by seating the guest on an overstuffed leather chair as Mirna re-entered the room. In accented English reflecting her Tuscan origins, Nonna Maria said, "I am here to visit the Sing Song Child. Several rooms near my office in the Angel School are being whitewashed and I do not like the smell, so I decided to visit some of the children and make sure they are keeping up with their studies." Nonna Maria leaned forward, teased Andrew's hair and added in a low voice, "And I want to make sure they are being fed and clothed properly. Most of all, that they are treated well." She brightened. "Of course, I know Andrew is loved and well taken care of, but I wanted to stop by anyway to visit. He is one of my favorite students. And I wanted to enlist you, Francisco and Mirna and now you, too, Alphonse and Chantal, to come up with stimulation for the students. They need it badly."

Just then Andrew and Crestina arrived and, with a cry, the lad reached for his teacher. Nonna Maria and Andrew embraced in a joyful hug, and Chantal could see tears in their eyes.

Teresa returned with a silver tray of smoked sausages, an assortment of flaky French cheese pastries, and a pitcher of hot tea sweetened with honey. Another servant added steins of ale and set them on the table.

Nonna Maria drank deeply from her stein and set the container on a hand-tooled leather coaster on the oval table in front of her. Mirna said, "Nonna Maria, the circus is visiting our town in one week and there is to be a parade the day before. What do you think of our approaching the local businesses and asking them for tickets so the students at the Angel School may attend?"

Nonna Maria looked down at the floor. "You know, they are quite in need of something besides their daily routine at school." She looked up and continued, "That's an excellent idea, Mirna, but I daresay there's not enough carriages in all of Whittleford to carry all our children to the show. But how marvelous it would be for them. Just think of all the animals.

The sounds and colors. The smell of peanuts, fresh sweet candy, and sawdust on the floor. The performances. The clowns. Simply being in the environment with all the excitement would be the perfect event to engage the children. The circus. The menagerie. How wonderful and magical would that be. Perfect for the children. Yes, but how to get the children to the circus?"

There was a momentary silence until a creak in the wooden floor behind the group attracted their attention.

A beaming Alphonse stood beside the two princes. Royalty. Francisco rose to greet his guests.

Prince Solomon's deep, baritone voice broke the quiet. "If you would please pardon the intrusion, my dear ladies and gentlemen. We overheard your discussion. There is no problem. No problem at all. The circus shall come to the Angel School. We shall have another parade, this time the procession will pass in front of the children. Is there a large, grassy, pasture or field adjacent to or in the vicinity of the school?"

Nonna Maria nodded.

The prince continued, "Then *there* is we shall have our traditional, season ending, grand finale performance ... for the children."

The excited group rose to thank the prince for his generosity.

Andrew bubbled and laughed, honking his horn over and over until shushed by Crestina.

At last, Francisco made himself heard above the hubbub. "Prince Solomon. And this must be Prince Samuel, the Prince of Clowns. So good to meet you," said Francisco as the others gathered around them. "Come in, come in. We did not hear your entrance." Introductions were made and everyone except Prince Samuel sat down once again.

Mirna said to him, "Sit down, Prince Samuel. You must be tired after the ride to *La Estancia*."

The prince declined, saying that he wanted to stretch his legs after the long carriage ride. He smiled and said, "And please call us by our given names of Solomon and Samuel. We are all equal in the eyes of the Lord."

Andrew was wide-eyed with the anticipation of the circus coming and meeting the Prince of Clowns. Finally, he could control himself no longer. "re ou a lown?"

Prince Samuel smiled and bent over the boy. Just as he was beginning to reply, he noticed the toy brass horn in Andrew's lap. He took the noisemaker and, holding the device up to his face with his right hand, examined the item closely as if for the first time. Quite by accident, he squeezed the horn's rubber, bulbous end and yelled when a loud honking sound came forth.

Yowling in terror, Ren jumped up and bolted for the kitchen.

Instead of dropping the noisemaker in alarm, Samuel pretended that the horn had come alive and was stuck to his hand. What's more, the horn kept honking and at the same time seemed intent on attaching itself like a leech to Samuel's neck.

The comedy unfolded in a flash. With his left hand Samuel tried to pry the mad device from his right hand while still keeping the instrument from assaulting his neck.

The struggle between man and horn continued for almost a minute until the scenario became apparent to all that he had no chance of either freeing the horn from his hand or stopping the noise making. Eyes bulging, the prince looked about the room with a look of sheer desperation on his face. As his eyes fell upon the couch, Samuel's expression quickly changed from desperation to hope.

With a sideways glance at the horn, he whispered the words, "I have a plan."

In a mock titanic test of strength, his left hand slowly subdued the right.

Then, in one swift motion his left hand shoved his right hand bearing the wildly honking horn under one of the large, soft cushions of the sofa.

The victorious Prince Samuel then quickly sat down on the cushion and exhaled in relief. Despite the muffled honking sounds still emanating from under the cushion, the prince affected an air of bored nonchalance as he straightened his tie with his left hand and pretended as if nothing had happened. After a few moments the sounds slowed, then stopped.

In a slow and cautious motion, the prince removed the inert horn from under the cushion.

At arm's length, he presented the horn back to Andrew, who eyed the suspicious device. Smiling, Samuel asked the dumbfounded boy, "A clown? Me? Why do you ask?"

The room burst into laughter at the expression on Andrew's face, still gaping at the performance.

When the excitement had subsided, Nonna Maria said to Prince Solomon, "On behalf of all the children and teachers at the Angel School, we thank you in advance for including us in your schedule. You probably will never know all the positive things your decision will do for the children. Many of them have bodies handicapped by injury or illness. Sadly, some have given up on life. The joy and excitement the circus provides will help them temporarily cope with their handicaps and brighten their day."

Prince Solomon grinned. "Not *my* decision to make, Nonna Maria. Samuel is in charge of the scheduling. When we overheard your heartfelt comments, he made an instant decision to help."

Nonna Maria said in a soft voice, "Goodness."

The future king addressed Nonna Maria, "Our circus loves families and especially children. *We,* the performers, are honored to perform for the children and teachers of the Angel School. I have but one request: a few hours before the first performance, introduce us in advance to each child who attends. We will entertain and show them we are not to be feared. We will show each of them they are loved no matter what they think of themselves. We call this 'own-portrait'. Many malformed children think they are not worthy of love."

He continued, "For those with handicapped bodies, well, we will try to relay to them the Biblical truth that they will have new bodies free of imperfections in Heaven if they become believers in the Lord and His salvation. We shall approach the audience at random to include them with others in the acts."

Teresa asked, "My curiosity has been piqued, Prince Samuel. Before I go to the kitchen to serve dinner, I have one question: why those children with low own-portrait?"

The prince explained, "Well, Teresa, there are a few reasons. When a person has a poor own-image, or *propira picturam* in the Greek, that way of thinking about themselves keeps them down by not letting them do and be all they can as a person. This is for both men and women. Their poor own-portrait keeps them from dreaming great dreams and chasing those dreams. They get discouraged and don't even *want* to try. Then they don't try at all; that lack of effort is the world's loss."

Nonna Maria observed, "Yes, Teresa, a poor own-portrait keeps people from having meaningful relationships with others as well. Many times people who feel bad about themselves build an emotional bastion to keep others out and to keep from feeling pain from rejection. This is a great tragedy. And think about this too: If people don't think well about themselves, this keeps them from serving the Lord and being happy in Him because they think they are not worthy of His love. Surely this is not what He wants. Especially for children."

Prince Samuel agreed, "Yet, this is not to say that we should all go around grinning like idiots or have an inflated opinion of ourselves. Certainly not. Our task is to see that people have a realistic own-portrait and recognize that, even though others may not share that opinion, God loves them regardless. You see? Their perspective must change to recognize that God is in control. Part of our training as clowns and performers in the Banouso and Wisbar Circus is to recognize such people, children or adults, and treat them with great gentleness and sensitivity, as God treats us even though we may not recognize it. Now, all people, no matter how miserable they are, want to be accepted by others. So, we try raising a person up by using humor and by including them in our skits. Humor and the good news of God's gentle love – these are powerful tools indeed. But sometimes a person is miserable because life has become too difficult for them to handle. God said in the Book of Matthew that we should give our troubles to the Lord Jesus in order that we should rest in Him. In fact, Jesus said that He wants to carry those burdens for us, to let Him be our strength. But sometimes, especially for adults, a person is miserable because he or she is not heeding God's will in their lives. For them, returning to His way is the only way they will truly feel good about themselves." Samuel paused and looked about the room. "The unspoken question is 'Does that mean that all the persons we approach to participate think themselves in a lowly way?' No, we include those with healthy propira picturam too. We circus members pray together as a group before each performance and ask the Lord to show us whom to include. God is marvelous. He hasn't failed us yet, and I am confident He never will. "

Teresa replied happily, "Yes, thank you for explaining, Prince Samuel, I understand. God never fails. I know this in my life too. But I must go and serve dinner. And I must rescue my kitchen from the dangers of Ren, the *gato*. *Perdoname, por favor*." With that, the feisty woman excused herself and left the room.

Samuel's smile returned and reminded Chantal of the performer in the marketplace earlier in the day. Chantal remarked, "Samuel, I believe we've met in an indirect way. You were the clown in the marketplace this morning, weren't you?" Prince Samuel grinned and confided, "Yes, that was me. I really enjoyed that performance. You know, I almost fell off the crate today." He laughed again. "The cord looped around my ankle at the most inopportune time. I'll have to work on that. No matter."

Sophie closed and rubbed her eyes for the fifth time in as many minutes to make the dream go away, but when she opened them she was still in her dream that really wasn't a dream. The girl was neck-deep in a tub full of warm, almost hot water. A most amazing creation, bubbles from soap, were floating on the water's surface. They even smelled of lavender, her favorite flower. She wished her stepsisters and brother could see her now and wondered how they were faring after that horrible time just two days ago. Sophie had walked towards the Angel School in drifts of snow that sometimes came up to mid-calf. She spent the first night under a rough jumble of branches that had offered concealment and some protection, but hadn't slept even a wink.

Sophie had then stumbled onward, eating the last of her cheese and milk, then drinking her fill of water on the bank of the river. It was afternoon when she had fallen on her knees in the middle of the road, unable to continue. Tears of fear and helplessness followed anguished prayers for help, and she failed to notice the slow, oddly dressed horse pulling a wagon approach from behind her. Through a fog of exhaustion she remembered being lifted to her feet, wrapped in a warm blanket and carried up to the bench of the wagon. And now here she was in a beautiful mansion being treated like family. No, like royalty. A bolt of fear stabbed through her stomach as a thought grabbed her; they will find out I'm an ugly, stupid peasant girl and throw me out like Stepfather did. Then she thought, but no–the Nonna Maria lady knows that and Francisco and Mirna still took me in. This is what Mother meant when she talked about what Jesus's friend James said to do – help orphans and widows.

A maid came in and washed her thoroughly, the water turning brown from the effort. Her hair was de-loused, then washed and dried then brushed until it shone like burnished gold. When she was dry, the maid dressed her in the most beautiful clothes she had ever seen.

After a while the maid left and she noticed her pottery and silver coin were laid out on table covered with a soft, white, silken cloth. Next to her possessions was a small, ornate silver cross on a fine silver chain. A selection of small meats, cheeses, and cooked vegetables was on a nearby table.

After devouring every morsel on the plate, Sophie sat on an adjacent chair, bowed her head in a prayer of thanks, and started to cry. In her exhaustion, this time she could not stop. Sleep came quickly. The head nurse, Yelli, carried the girl to a small, warm storage room hastily converted to a bedchambers, tucked her between the sparkling white linen sheets of a goose down duvet comforter and bid her pleasant dreams. She then sat down on a comfortable chair at the foot of the bed and took out a bag of knitting.

Chapter Thirteen
Afternoon into Evening

As Mirna and Chantal continued a lively conversation with Prince Samuel about their development of the Torrie Rose, Alphonse, Francisco, Andrew and Prince Solomon moved to the far corner of the room. Nonna Maria excused herself to look in on Sophie. The four sat at a beautiful, polished mahogany table and chair set that had been in Francisco's family many generations.

Alphonse set his wineglass on a leather coaster and said to Prince Solomon, "So, old friend, the years have been kind to you, but you have many more years to come. What are your future intentions? You spoke of opportunity in the Gingerbread House."

Prince Solomon laughed in his deep baritone voice, and then grew serious. He replied, "Opportunity. Yes, there is much opportunity for those with imagination and drive. Indeed, this topic is the reason for my visit. You, Francisco are no longer working, and you and I, Alphonse, will stop working shortly. I believe, yes, that there is life yet in these old bones."

Alphonse and Francisco laughed, and Prince Solomon continued in earnest, "Our affection for and our dedication to the confectionery trade is unmatched. We have a genuine love of what we do. In that regard, we three possess many decades of experience in the business.

From my perspective as Prime Director of the United Confectionery House, I have dealt with you gentlemen many times, both in business and in person. I have been a guest in your homes as you both have been guests in mine and have found you both to be men of honor and principle. Therefore, I propose that the three of us join together and form our own venture, not in production, but specializing in the transport of goods. We would each bring a complimentary expertise."

The prince opened a leather valise and passed a stack of paper to Alphonse and Francisco. "Please examine these applications and plans I have had drawn up and see if you are interested in joining as my equal partners in such an effort."

Francisco cleared his throat as if to speak. He was quieted by a small gesture of Alphonse's hand and the interested, thoughtful look on Alphonse's face that seemed to say, "Let's hear the rest of this before we respond."

The older man took his cue from the younger and kept whatever thoughts he had to himself.

The prince noticed the exchange but continued, "Consider what I propose. Opportunity. But we must not delay. There are new trade laws subtly favoring countries neighboring Deltanos. The King of Tierary has created his own. There are two countries neighboring Tierary that will start the same this New Year. The end of the year is in two months. I am to leave for my estate in two weeks; travel time to Deltanos is one month and one week. If we start our partnership two weeks and one day from now, I can hurry back to Deltanos next week and begin the paperwork. Examine the documents and let us modify what we must. All that is required is your signatures."

Alphonse and Francisco remained silent for a moment, digesting all that the prince had said. They took several minutes to examine and contemplate the papers in front of them. Francisco bent down and showed each document to the ever-attentive Andrew.

Alphonse felt Chantal's warm, familiar hand on his shoulder and smiled to himself without taking his eyes from the page. After a while he looked up and noticed Mirna and Prince Samuel had joined the group. An angel stood at Mirna's elbow. He waved at Alphonse and vanished. Surprised, Alphonse shook his head a little and with an effort, resumed reading. Finally, Francisco rose and looked back at Alphonse and Andrew, both of whom nodded and smiled in agreement.

Francisco said, "Solomon, these two sets of creaky old bones *have* considered these new laws. Alphonse, Andrew and I are forming a new business to take advantage of our experience and contacts *todo el mundo*, worldwide. Over the span of the last several months, we have been planning this venture. One month ago, we completed the application, but an important piece of the leadership still seemed missing." He paused and smiled. "Indeed, difficult was the task to find that missing ingredient because at first glance our endeavor was complete. But each of us had an unsettled feeling, which lingered on despite our efforts to remedy the situation.

"Three weeks ago, we just gave up and started praying for the Lord's will in our company. Last night we found the missing piece."

Alphonse interjected, "Actually, the missing piece came to us. *You*, old chap. We've prayed about this decision and believe that your proposal is the Lord's answer to those prayers. These applications and the business ideas you have given us are virtually identical with those we sent off. Indeed, the coincidence is beyond amazing. This morning, courtesy of Snorffleham Palace, we have sent a speedy band of couriers to process the documents for a new trade based in Deltanos and Tierary effective the day before New Year's."

Francisco walked to a desk on the side of the room and retrieved his valise. Rummaging about inside, he withdrew a simple, worn leather folder containing a stack of official-looking documents. Opening the folder, he handed them to the prince and said, "See here, *amigo*. Your name is prominent as possible partner. Now that we know that you wish to work with us, we merely add another document announcing your position as full partner with Alphonse, Andrew and myself when you are next in Deltanos. At your leisure, I might add. *Bienvenidos*. Welcome to the partnership, my friend."

Prince Solomon looked stunned for a moment and said in an emotion-choked voice, "I am deeply honored. Let us give thanks to the Lord."

And with that, three men, three ladies and one little boy bowed their heads and humbly praised the Lord for His wisdom and grace.

Teresa joined the praying group at a respectful distance until the impromptu prayer session had ended to announce, "Dinner is served." She then placed Ren, smelling of garlic and chives, in Andrew's lap and kissed the boy's cheek. "Your little *gato* likes roast duckling, I think. Cream too." Everyone chuckled as Ren licked a paw, groomed his whiskers and settled down for a nap in Andrew's lap.

Nonna Maria rejoined the group and quietly told Mirna that her young guest was asleep.

As one, the group moved into the dining room to find an exquisite table setting featuring scrumptious dishes from Deltanos and Tierary. Mirna, Chantal and Teresa had worked together to prepare each dish, using only the freshest spices and herbs from their garden and the finest produce from Tierary's market.

Their culinary prowess became evident when each course was uncovered. The centerpiece was a decorative display of daisies, asters and baby's breath flowers. Chantal and Mirna had grown each plant from seeds in their hothouses.

As they moved to their seats, the princes and Nonna Maria marveled at their beauty.

When each person was settled, Francisco said the blessing. Andrew insisted on being seated between Nonna Maria and Prince Samuel.

Francisco led the group in a prayer of thanks-giving for the Lord's bounty, while servants busied themselves around the table.

An excellent French Chardonnay was served in fragile crystal glasses, as Francisco stood and cleared his throat.

"*Amigos y amigas*, let us toast the moment by remembering words of wisdom spoken long ago, but meaningful in these modern times."

The others raised their glasses. Andrew raised his mug with Samuel's assistance.

Ren stood, stretched, then jumped down from Andrew's lap and padded toward the kitchen.

Francisco chuckled and said, "Ah, little Ren. We probably served the wrong beverage."

He continued,

> "May you never lie, cheat, steal or drink.
> But if you must lie, then lie only in the

arms of the one you love.
If you must cheat, then only cheat death.
If you must steal then only steal away from bad company.
And if you must drink, then only drink in the
moments that take your breath away."

Voices rose in unison, "Hear, hear."
Francisco took his seat as servants refilled the glasses.
Prince Samuel stood, raised his glass, and said, "As you know, Deltanos is a seafaring nation. Generations ago this toast arrived on our shores from parts unknown, but like Francisco's salute, is still relevant indeed."

'There are good ships,
and there are wooden ships,
and ships that sail the sea.
But the best ships, are *friendships*,
and may they always be'. "

"Well done, Samuel. Well done."
As the courses were being served, Mirna asked Nonna Maria how she had chosen teaching as her career.
In her Tuscan accent, Nonna Maria replied, "But teaching is what I have always wanted to do. I was inspired by one of my grade-school teachers to do my best at my studies, and to help another student if we understood a concept and someone else did not. I seemed to be good at explaining things to others and found doing this rewarding in my heart. I decided to find a job in teaching, helping those who need a little more help in their education. *Mama miá*, a job that turned out to be so much more than that. That's my story. Please pass the salad, Prince Solomon."

Smiling, Prince Solomon handed her the cobalt-blue glass serving bowl and said, "Here you are, Nonna Maria. But, please explain; in what way has your job become more than a career?"

Turning to face the prince, she reflected to herself for a moment, then continued, "Well, my good Solomon, many years ago, my first teaching position came when economic times were difficult in my country. The only spot open was teaching a group of children who had needs different from their peers. I accepted the offer because I had taken some courses in this area in University. My ability to speak three other languages certainly helped. On the last week of the first part of my first year my heart melted and I dedicated my career to helping children."

She shrugged expansively. "Now I am Headmistress over the Angel School and involved with another. Who was to know? My career has become my life. I spend my earnings caring for my children. I buy clothes, shoes, socks, undergarments, hats, jackets and whatever food they need. I take them on my vacations and many times they sleep at my house. The Throne helps and Francisco and Mirna have been very generous, but many, many times I am all there is between them and their having no one and nowhere to go. Like Sophie whom I found today I simply will not say "no" to a child in need. She is asleep, yes? Such a darling girl. Her stepfather kicked her out two days ago. Well, no more pulling potatoes for her. If she wants, she shall live with us at the Angel School from here on. She shall receive an education, proper nutrition and a safe place to grow up."

Alphonse noticed Andrew's eyes brighten at the mention of a peasant girl "pulling potatoes" and smiled, for Andrew had told him about the girl in the field.

Nonna Maria continued, "But let me tell you that I alone am not enough. I always pray for my little angels and ask the Lord to provide and protect them each day. We don't have much, but we have all that we need. Trusting in the Lord is enough. The Lord provides."

Looking at Samuel, she said, "Your generosity with the circus will be so much appreciated, Prince Samuel. Thank you again."

Intrigued, the prince answered, "You are quite welcome. Giving is what we must do, Nonna Maria, indeed, it is the *right* thing to do. But, if I may, what caused your heart to melt on that day? I don't mean to pry, but surely you knew what you were getting into."

Nonna Maria paused then answered, "No, not really, my dear prince. I loved my job, but my occupation was merely a job none-the-less – until the day of the great snow. My class had become the first stop for many immigrant children into my country. On that day, though, a little boy of about five years' old came to me in tears. His name was Tomás and he was in my class his second day off the vessel that had carried him and his family to Tuscany. *Pobrecito niño*, the poor little darling came to me crying his heart out. He seemed frightened and hugged my leg with all his little might. I dried his tears and asked him what was wrong. He explained that it had turned very cold outside and there were cold white feathers the size of a peso falling from the sky. I looked outside and it was snowing. Hard. I sat down, gathered him up on my lap and explained 'snow' to him. Tomás said that he was afraid that if he got lost on his way home, he would starve.

I asked him why and he told me that the white feathers from Heaven were covering the houses and the trees. If he got lost he wouldn't be able to find any fruit to eat on the trees in the neighborhood. Then my heart melted and I knew that the children were my purpose in life."

The room had grown quiet.

Alphonse cleared his throat with a soft "harrumph" and looked away with a lump in his throat, preoccupied with something in his eye.

Francisco turned to Alphonse, leaned toward him slightly and said under his breath, "You old softie." But Alphonse noticed a bit of moisture in the corner of Francisco's eyes, too.

Prince Solomon took Nonna Maria's hand in his own and, eyes shining, kissed her hand gently. "You are a marvelous woman indeed, Nonna Maria. I am honored to have made your acquaintance."

Nonna Maria blushed and said, "I am nothing but God's servant, Prince Solomon. But thank you for your kind words."

Dinner lasted late into the evening. The excellent food, fascinating stories, good-natured banter and pleasant company made the time pass quickly. Francisco and Mirna had put Andrew to bed hours before, the tired but happy boy having lost the struggle to stay awake.

The hour was getting late, and everyone pitched in to clear the table.

Alphonse stifled a yawn as he and Chantal stacked the dirty dishes onto serving trays. Prince Solomon and Nonna Maria carried them into the kitchen. Francisco, Mirna, and Prince Samuel teamed up to wash and dry the dishes and made quick work of the items brought to them.

The group gathered in the kitchen as the last of the dinner dishes was washed, dried and put away. Prince Samuel remarked, "Francisco and Mirna, dinner was excellent. You have lived up to what Solomon told me of your hospitality. On a personal note, I am pleased with the way dinner was prepared and served. One would think that with your vast holdings that you would have servants doing these tasks. I am gratified to see people unspoiled by wealth."

Francisco said quietly, "We dismissed the servants hours ago so they could take their rest. They have families and lives as well, you know, and their lives are as precious to them as ours to us. As you and Solomon said hours ago, we are equals in the eyes of the Lord. We must keep that perspective in the forefront of our minds. Serving ourselves and cleaning up after ourselves helps to reinforce that."

Samuel pointed to a spot on his tunic and sighed, "Yes, but let's hope someone knows how to remove stains from this fabric. I was a bit careless on the cleanup."

Nonna Maria snorted and said, "Spoken just like a helpless man. Young Samuel, give your tunic in the morning and I shall take care of this. They do not call me 'Nonna' for nothing."

The group laughed, bid each other good night and headed off their separate ways to turn in.

A full moon provided pale illumination as the men from Deltanos closed the back door, drew their cloaks closer to themselves to ward off the cold wind and started for the guesthouse.

Their accommodations lay on the far side of a large, rectangular garden. Row upon row of healthy, green, vibrant Torrie Rose plants were lit in the yellowish orange light of two dozen flickering oil lamps.

The two princes paused for a moment to savor the garden's beauty.

"They're beautiful," remarked Prince Solomon.

"Breathtaking," agreed Prince Samuel, who continued, "Look about, Solomon. The rest of the landscape is readying itself for winter. Trees without leaves, grasses and shrubs brown and dead. But the Torries are just now getting started. Imagine. Roses in winter. Look at how beautiful they are even now. And these aren't even in bud yet." He wondered out loud, "However did they accomplish such a thing?"

Prince Solomon answered the younger man, "I do not know. I heard you discussing their development today. Have you approached them about developing a Torrie for Deltanos? Surely if they can get roses to prosper in the frigid Tierarian winter they can get Torries to prosper in the withering heat of a Deltanosian summer."

Prince Samuel replied, "No, I've not asked yet. Tomorrow, perhaps during breakfast or if we tour the hothouses, the proper time will come." He paused. "Say, were they cold houses for the Torries?"

Prince Solomon grinned, "Will they be 'very-hothouses' for us?" They both laughed at their inside joke.

Prince Samuel glanced at the sky, sniffed the frosty night air and said, "We're in for a change of weather soon. Perhaps as early as tomorrow morning. More snow, but this time the accumulation will stay for a few days. I hope the snow will be absorbed into the ground by the time we are to perform in Whittleford. No matter. Winter has begun. Soon those amazing roses will bloom. I do miss my beloved Deltanos, but soon my favorite time of the year in Tierary will be here."

Prince Solomon replied, "Yes, mine too, but let us be on our way. This has been a long day."

The two turned and continued toward the guest house and the warm, comfortable beds they were sure were waiting.

At the same time the princes were conversing in the rose garden, Alphonse and Mirna had walked up the stairs and had just turned the corner to the corridor leading to the guest chambers.

Alphonse, in the lead, was carrying a candle enclosed in a glass globe for illumination, with Chantal holding her own candle not far behind. For the barest of moments, he could clearly see golden light streaming from under Andrew's door. Then the light winked out. Unable to believe his eyes, Alphonse turned to Chantal, pointed to the now unlit passageway and exclaimed excitedly, "Chantal. I say. Chantal. Did you see that? I saw it again. Light. From underneath Andrew's door."

Chantal stifled a yawn and replied, "No, I saw nothing, but I am so tired that I was following you with my eyes half closed. Darling, let's go to bed. We can discuss your imaginings in the morning."

The two continued down the hallway, with Alphonse glancing back down the corridor as he was about to enter their room. To his dismay, Andrew's doorway remained dark.

A partly opened window had made their room as chilly as the outside. Chantal quickly shut the offending portal and drew the heavy drapes designed to ward off the cold. Alphonse stoked the banked coals and added several pieces of wood to the fireplace. Soon, warm yellow firelight from dancing flames had taken the chill off the room. The couple readied themselves to retire for the evening.

"Good heavens, I'm freezing," shivered Chantal, as she peeled back the duvet and slipped between the crisp linen sheets.

"Brrrrrr," agreed Alphonse, as he joined his wife. In haste, he pulled the covers back over them both and, laughing, they sought each other's body heat and sweet delight. Under the shelter of the night, the main house eventually fell into deep slumber. But morning's gentle insistence overcame the darkness and all too soon daybreak returned.

14
Chapter Fourteen
Morning

Alphonse awoke first in the dimly lit room and with-out moving, looked over at his wife. Chantal was on her side, facing him. Her breathing was deep and constant. The down-filled covers were tucked up to her chin; loose tendrils of her shoulder length silky auburn hair had cascaded in a careless way onto the white pillowcase and created a beautiful ornate pattern. Here and there Alphonse noticed her hair was becoming tinged with gray, and that the laugh wrinkles on the corner of her eyes had grown and deepened. He thought back to the many good times and some not-so-happy times that they had seen and felt his heart brimming with even more love for her than before.

She chuckled in her sleep; remnants perhaps of laughter from the night before. As he watched her still, sleeping form, a gentle rat-a-tat-tat sound came from the door.

Chantal stirred, yawned and said in a sleepy voice, "That must be Teresa, my love. Let us enjoy breakfast in bed. This is my treat. You stay put, I'll answer the door."

Alphonse smiled as Chantal kissed him lightly on the lips, then stood, stretched and put on her warm robe and slippers. He burrowed deeper under the toasty covers as she stoked the hearth to produce a flame, then lit a pair of candles from a small brand.

"I'll be right there, Teresa," called Chantal as she hurried over to the door. With a quick look backward at Alphonse she then opened the door, expecting to find the cook with a covered silver platter. Instead, a grinning Andrew looked up from his wheelchair.

He said, "Ood orning, *Tiá* antal."

Chantal bent over and gave the youth a hug and kissed him on the cheek. Smiling, she said, "Andrew. Why hello, nephew. What a pleasant surprise. Good morning to you as well."

Andrew giggled and pointed to the heavily covered window and said, "Ow, ucho ow."

Chantal wheeled Andrew into the chamber and beckoned Alphonse to the window. "Snow?"

She threw open the drapes and was pleasantly surprised to find the outside covered by a deepening blanket of clean, white snow. Large, thick flakes were still falling and the leaden gray sky was heavy with the possibility of more.

Andrew leaned forward in his wheelchair and, eyes bright, said in a soft, hushed voice, "Wow."

Alphonse stretched in bed and rose to put on his robe and slippers. He walked across the cold, creaky wooden floor, joining his wife and Andrew at the window. He tousled Andrew's hair before giving him a hug and kiss on the cheek.

Alphonse chuckled and said, "Good morning, partner. I see you brought us good news. Snow. I say, old chap, I have a fabulous idea. Ask your parents: Let's me, you, *Tia* Chantal, your parents and the two princes go for a toboggan ride or two down *Mañana* Hill after breakfast. Then we can go to *La Casita* after tobogganing, just like we always do. Maybe Nonna Maria would like to go too. Like that idea?"

The excited Andrew nodded his head several times and handed Alphonse a small envelope with a handwritten note inside.

Alphonse handed the note to Chantal, who opened and read the document out loud, "Good morning, sleepyheads. We have been up for an hour. Our Sing Song Child wanted to wake you for breakfast before lunch is to be served. Please join us in the kitchen at your convenience."

Chantal looked at Alphonse in disbelief and said, "Do you know the time? We must have slept much later than we planned."

A voice from the open doorway said, "Good morning. Pardon the intrusion, but daybreak has come and gone."

Alphonse and Chantal turned and greeted Crestina, who walked over to Andrew's wheeled chair.

Crestina said, "If this young man is to play in the snow as your father and mother have planned, he must be properly fueled for the day. Come, Andrew, first brunch, and then play."

Alphonse said, "That's right. The first snowfall of the year. Tradition must be maintained. *Mañana* Hill. And then *La Casita* for dinner afterwards. Crestina, would you like to join us?"

Crestina thoughtfully replied, "I shall accompany you, not to the Hill, but certainly for dinner. I have already spoken to *Don* Francisco and *Doña* Mirna. My sister, Angeline, shall arrive this afternoon. She is to be Andrew's speech teacher and physical therapist and is quite excited to be having him for a student. Angeline has developed several new techniques for improving a person's motor coordination and could perhaps help Andrew's condition. Doña Chantal, Angeline is also an avid gardener and hopes to learn much from you and Doña Mirna."

Chantal said graciously, "I have heard of Angeline's skills with children. I cannot wait to meet her. I would be delighted to teach her all that I know. The world needs more people who love to tend and cultivate plants."

Crestina smiled and wheeled a happy Andrew from the room, saying, "See you in the kitchen."

Alphonse closed the door and stoked the fire in the fireplace, adding several pieces of wood. As the room warmed, he and Chantal bathed and dressed.

They then read Psalm 23 from Alphonse's bible, prayed together and thus were ready to start their day.

In another room, Yelli conferred with Nonna Maria and Mirna. During the night, Sophie had developed a high fever. She had thrashed about all night, calling out for her brother, Rhys, to protect her and trying to get away from a horror named 'Sefada Woosey'. "I don't know who this 'Sefada Woosey' is, but we must keep her away from Andrew till her fever abates and she is no longer ill. And for several days after the fever subsides. We cannot afford for him to become ill. Not now." Yelli told the ladies. "I can handle whatever illness she may have, but under no circumstances must Sophie and he have any contact whatsoever. Their initial meeting should be at the Angel School. And, speaking about Andrew, somehow he seems a bit *different* don't you think? Not just more mature. Perhaps it is because he is getting older, but he seems *changed* in some way I cannot put my finger on."

Mirna smiled. "Yes. He's growing up into a fine young man."

15
Chapter Fifteen
Breakfast

Alphonse and Chantal descended the stairway and followed the pungent, inviting coffee aroma coming from the kitchen. Seated at the table behind four heavy porcelain mugs of steaming coffee were Samuel, Solomon, Andrew, and Francisco. Although each man had clean-shaven faces and neatly combed hair, the sleepy looks on their faces showed that they had not been up for long.

Andrew smiled as the couple entered the kitchen. Mirna, wearing a robin's egg blue apron around her waist and a smudge of brown wheat flour on her chin was standing, facing the large wood-burning stove. She smiled and waved.

"Good morning," said Alphonse and Chantal.

"Good morning," the men answered in one voice.

"Coffee, my dear?" said Alphonse to his wife.

Chantal smiled and nodded in the affirmative.

Alphonse walked over to the silver coffee urn and took two mugs from the counter. He then poured a generous portion of coffee into each. One mug became the recipient of cream and sugar; the others contents remained undisturbed. He handed one of the mugs to Chantal, who rewarded him with a small kiss on the cheek.

"Thank you, Alphonse," said Chantal. She held her mug in both hands, drank deeply of the heady aroma, then took a dainty sample of the hot beverage. "Mmmmm. Wonderful. Coffee. Black. Next to algebra and sailing, black coffee is one of the wonders of the civilized world."

Taking a sip from his own mug, Alphonse said in a bright voice, "I say, chin up. Pip Pip. Cheerio. Good morning, good morning," and seated himself opposite from Francisco.

Alphonse looked at Francisco and continued, "I'm beginning to like the idea of a mug of hot, strong coffee in the morning, my friend. Especially with the snow falling so hard outside. I say, that reminds me. The 'Hill', right?"

Francisco laughed and replied, "The 'Hill'? *Por supueseto.* Of course, *amigo.* Tradition must be observed. As for coffee, yes, I can tell of your growing fondness for the bean. A hot mug of coffee certainly does have a good taste in the morning."

Francisco then gestured to the untouched silver tea set on the counter and said to Alphonse, "So I'm not surprised that you didn't have your usual morning Oolong tea."

Alphonse smilingly replied, "I say, old chap, when one finds himself in Rome…"

Everyone laughed. Just then Nonna Maria walked into the kitchen and set her oversized purse on the floor. She grinned and said in her heavy accent, "Ah, *Roma.* The golden city on seven hills. The sparkling jewel in the world's crown. *Mama mia.* The center of the known universe. The world revolves around the beck and call of Europe's finest city. Ah, *Roma,*" and further extolled Rome's virtues with a brief, flowing dance.

The others laughed and cheered, applauding her dexterity and fluid grace.

When she was through, Nonna Maria took a mug and poured herself some coffee, adding a dollop of cream and one tiny spoonful of sugar.

Nonna Maria wagged a finger at the group and warned, "Too much sugar is bad for you."

She then started to take a seat at the table to the right of Prince Solomon.

The prince jumped up from his chair and insisted on pushing in the chair for Nonna Maria.

"Thank you, Prince Solomon," she said with a smile, "You are a true gentleman."

Prince Solomon laughed but then returned to his seat and said, "As infants, we are born without knowledge and appreciation of social graces. Even for something as simple as assisting at the table. As a teacher, you know, manners are taught, Nonna Maria. My parents were strict but loving and insisted that adults be treated as such. They required me, my brothers, and my sisters to act in a respectful manner toward elders, especially toward women. Your kind words are a tribute and compliment to them, not me. As a youth, I can recall many times having received the "rod of correction" on my "seat of understanding". Ha. But beforehand and in a calm way, my parents explained why we were going to be disciplined. In retrospect this was an excellent idea because we sometimes had forgotten the incident or didn't know that we had done wrong. The corporal punishment they administered was always with love and always with forgiveness afterward. Never with anger. As a result, my siblings and I turned out well. The King and Queen of Deltanos, Prince Samuel's father and mother, discipline their children the same way."

The elder prince laughed, shook his head and continued, "Which proves once again that the bible is right in teaching us how to raise our children."

Chantal donned an apron hanging from a peg on the wall, and turned to help her friend. Mirna gestured to a large, wooden mixing bowl on the counter and said, "Would you be a dear and stir that mixture up a bit more? Perhaps this could use a bit more dill."

"Of course, Mirna," replied Chantal. Picking up the mixing bowl, she sniffed the concoction and added just a pinch of the herb as Mirna also went about the task of preparing the meal. Soon, the mouth-watering aromas coming from the stove and oven made one and all more than ready to eat.

Mirna and Chantal had to shoo the inquisitive Francisco and Alphonse from sampling the breakfast dishes and offering to help. Finally, Mirna put them to work setting the table.

Prince Solomon snickered and said, "Setting the table is the proper penalty for spending too much time next to the stove, gentlemen. My mother would be proud."

Mirna turned, looked at Prince Solomon and teased, "Well, sir, to keep you from chortling *too* much, why don't you and Samuel visit the root cellar and choose the jams and marmalades? Francisco can show you the way when he is finished setting the table."

Chantal added, "And we could use a bit more wood for the fire, Alphonse."

The men fled the kitchen.

With a triumphant laugh Mirna turned to Chantal and said, "Too many cooks spoil the breakfast."

Andrew sat silently in his wheelchair, eyes wide.

Mirna noticed the quiet youth. Assuming a mock stern look on her face, she captured his attention with her eyes and walked toward him with a large serving spoon holding a bit of food. Mirna said, "And for you, mister smarty, stop your staring this instant ... and taste this piece of sausage for me, will you?"

Relieved, the youth laughed as he sampled the treat. "MMMmmmm," was all that he could muster as Mirna tenderly placed a kiss on the top of his head and then lowered the spoon to Ren, who started licking it.

Soon the men reappeared and regained their seats at the table.

Francisco turned to the royals and said, "Oh, I almost forgot to mention, *amigos*, that we have a tradition here at *La Estancia*. We celebrate the first heavy accumulation of snow by setting aside a morning and afternoon for enjoying a winter picnic and tobogganing down *Mañana* Hill. Tobogganing is really fun. Care to join us?"

After a moment, Prince Samuel replied, "I would be delighted, Francisco. But may I ask what is tobogganing?"

After a moment, the laughter of disbelief erupted from those around the table.

When the hubbub had subsided, Prince Solomon grinned sheepishly and admitted also, "Tobogganing. Toboggans. Although I have heard of them, I have not seen one. I understand their function is similar to that of a sled."

This time the laughter grew, with Andrew honking his horn and snickering with glee.

Alphonse took a sip of his coffee and said to Prince Samuel, "I say, old chap, you really do not know what a toboggan is? Then indeed, the time has arrived for you to become acquainted with one. You too, Solomon. Your age does not disqualify you, as Francisco and I are equally challenged."

The elder prince smiled, shrugged and spoke. "Count me in, Alphonse. I shall live life to the fullest. *Carpe diem*." Solomon turned to Prince Samuel and said, "*Et tu*, Samuel?"

Prince Samuel snorted and said, "Count me in too, cousin. I am also curious about this toboggan device. I must know what all the fuss is about."

Francisco grinned at Prince Samuel and said, "*Amigo*, to truly *know* the toboggan you must *experience* the toboggan. Then the matter is settled. I, as your host, will ride with you. We must make your first toboggan ride down *Mañana* Hill a memorable one."

Mirna interrupted. "Me, too. This should be fun."

Alphonse turned and looked at Nonna Maria. "And you, Nonna Maria? Are you to be left out of this adventure?"

Nonna Maria chuckled, "*Mama mia*. No, even though I used to ride my family's toboggan when I was a young girl, I think I have seen too many years for such activity. Besides, I must remain with Sophie."

Mirna said, "Nonna, Sophie is in good hands here at *La Estancia*. There's nothing you can do for her that Yelli cannot do, and Yelli has her own resources here that you do not. Let her rest and regain her strength here and you come with us to *Mañana* Hill for your own recuperation. Time away from duties is restorative, you know." Nonna Maria protested for a minute then relented when confronted with the logic and common sense of the situation. She paused, then with a smile on her face and a twinkle in her eye, "So be it. I will visit Sophie and if she is awake I will tell her she can trust this home." She laughed, "I too must witness this historic event, if only from the warm comfort of the sleigh at the bottom of the Hill."

Everyone chortled as Prince Samuel turned and said to Prince Solomon, "Whatever have we gotten ourselves into?"

At last the meal was ready. Francisco led the group in thanking the Lord for His bounty and asked Him to bless their day.

Mirna and Chantal then served a delightful, three-cheese soufflé, tasty pan-fried potatoes mixed with peppers, spices, and chunks of sausage. Thick slices of fresh baked, rough, dark bread laden with whipped butter and the prince's choices of sweet homemade jams and marmalades were washed down with chilled, fresh orange juice and more coffee.

Good-natured banter went back and forth across the table and the two princes commented again and again how much they enjoyed the meal. At last, the repast was over, and Francisco filled each person's coffee cup one more time.

Mirna addressed Solomon, Samuel, and Nonna Maria. "Chantal and I must check on a project we are working on; we cannot think of a better time to for you to tour our hothouses. Although snow is falling outside, we can use the underground passageways to avoid having to bundle up. There are warm jackets, scarves, and boots at our first stop — the study house, for walking outside in the snow, though."

Nonna Maria said, "I must return to my room for a moment to get a warmer cloak for the underground walk and check on Sophie. I am cold-natured. I shall meet you at the entrance to the walk," and disappeared down the hallway.

Prince Samuel spoke first, "Seeing your growing facilities is a capital idea, Mirna. And being given a personal tour by the Mothers of the Torrie Rose creators is a great honor indeed. Let us clean up the breakfast dishes at once."

Alphonse and Francisco looked at each other.

Alphonse turned back to Mirna and said, "No, no, start the tour without us, gentlemen. We shall tidy the kitchen and join you when we are done. And after the tour, *Mañana* Hill."

16
Chapter Sixteen
Marvels and Wonders

Mirna and Chantal led Nonna Maria and the two princes down the stairs leading to the cellar. Instead of continuing straight into the room, they turned left and entered an unheated underground passageway leading from the main house to the study house. There was a noticeable chill in the air. The neatly tiled floor led off into the distance. Although there were no oil lamps or candles offering illumination, one could easily read from a printed page.

Nonna Maria was the first to notice that the light seemed to come from nowhere but everywhere. "How can this be?" she wondered aloud. "I know we are walking underground but there is as much light as if we are walking in daylight. Where does the illumination come from?"

Mirna turned, and still walking, said, "From the walls. From the light-roses."

Noticing the look of confusion on her guest's face, she elaborated, "I'm sorry, I should explain. One night when we first set out to develop the Torrie Rose, Chantal had to return to the hothouse office to retrieve some notes. She noticed a dim white light coming from the far side of one of the hothouses and thought that someone had left a small, lit candle. As Chantal approached the light she realized that the illumination did not come from a candle but that one of our hybrid roses was giving off a pale white glow in the dark. Chantal came back to the main house and we worked on increasing the flower's light. Interestingly, as the amount of light increased, the size of the plant decreased. The illumination that you enjoy is from the result of those efforts. The walls and ceiling of the passageway are coated with a thin paste of nutrients, which nourishes the light-rose. We introduced the plants to the nutrients and they have flourished. Their growth is slow and although we are underground and the passageway is sealed, a small amount of moisture seeps in from outside and makes the air somewhat humid. This provides almost all the water the plants need. Aside from a little extra misting now and again, each plant is self-sustaining."

Prince Samuel took out a small magnifying glass from his pocket and examined the wall. To his amazement, he noticed tiny maroon roses giving off a soft white glow from the underside of their leaves and petals. In a hushed voice he said, "Astounding. Simply amazing. I believe that's called *bioluminescence*. From the Latin language, with 'bio' meaning 'life' and 'luminescence' meaning 'light-giving'. Light from life. In this case, light from roses. I studied about that and I have seen this at night in a ship's dim wake while at sea, but the scientific world's understanding is nothing compared to this."

Nonna Maria said, "This is a new subject to me. Where did you learn about that, Samuel?"

Prince Samuel replied, "Darby."

Chantal observed, "I know of Darby. A fine university noted for academic excellence."

Prince Solomon said, "Yes, Darby's academic programs provided me an outstanding education. But, ladies, don't you realize that your discovery could greatly advance scientific understanding in this area?"

Mirna continued, "Yes, but with the success of the Torrie Rose, we took the phenomenon for granted. The light-roses were fun developing, but we thought of them as an oddity because we were concentrating on other things. We had a product in need of an application until Francisco had the underground passageways constructed so we may walk to the hothouses without bundling up during our frigid winters that he thought of this practical use. Then we simply experimented a bit and *voila´* let there be light. Unfortunately, we have been unable to duplicate this elsewhere. But they are indeed beautiful." She smiled. "Andrew loves being here. He laughs and says that plants giving off light are like his being able to sing. A miracle happened for the plants to glow and sparkle, and a miracle will take place someday to make him sing."

Mirna paused for a moment, then continued sadly, "And sometimes he seems so close...." As Mirna's words trailed off, Nonna Maria put her arm around her friend's shoulder for comfort and support.

Chantal said, "Once a year, a really amazing thing happens. All the light-rose plants' petals and leaves fall off in about an hour on one day. As the petals drift to the floor, they sparkle and release a sweet, intense fragrance. The passageway walls and ceiling then becomes dark but the tile walkway looks like a hundred billion tiny stars has fallen on the ground. To be in the middle of the fall, to have the petals softly fall on you and all around you, to become part of the sparkle and the fragrance, that experience is one of the most wonderful, beautiful things I have ever experienced. We never miss that time. Francisco calls the phenomenon the 'Fall of Stars'. You are all quite welcome to join us next month."

Prince Solomon smiled, "Yes, I should like to join you on that day. Next month? I shall arrange my schedule around such an event."

Prince Samuel and Nonna Maria agreed that they, too, would like to experience the fall of the sparkling petals.

The group progressed further into the passageway and presently came to a small room with wooden stairs alongside a gently sloping ramp leading upwards.

As one, they tromped upstairs and into a warm, tidy room containing overloaded shelves of reference books and drawings of various flowers and plants. On one side of the room was a closed door. Against another wall was a large stone fireplace with a tiny but welcoming fire burning.

Mirna said, "We call this building the Study House. This is the sitting room where we keep records of our creations and consider new ideas. We spend much time here. Our husbands were very patient while we were here developing the Torrie. Many, many nights and days. Their patience is proof again of their love for us."

Prince Solomon chuckled and said, "Yes, the bible says 'love is patient' …"

Prince Samuel walked over to the fire and warmed his hands. He said, "And I notice that you have your bible here, too. That's good. This fire feels good. Quite thoughtful of your servants to have a fire going when we came in."

Chantal said, "This fire has been burning since early last week, Solomon. We developed a small tree that has bark and wood that burns with ease and for a very long time. The flames are difficult to extinguish. We keep one of them for research and another for heating the lab and the main house. Snorffleham Palace has asked us not to cultivate any more for the time being."

Surprised, Nonna Maria asked, "Why not? I would think that this tree would be a great benefit to the world."

Mirna answered, "Yes, but it could also be quite dangerous if it were to grow freely in the outdoors. It would pose a great hazard across the countryside. Could you imagine forest fires that last for weeks, if not months? Besides, the moratorium is only until we find a way to extinguish the flames quickly, easily and..." Mirna's sentence was interrupted by rapid, heavy sounds of clomping footsteps coming up the stairs.

"Hallooo up there," echoed Francisco's voice as he and Alphonse neared the top of the stairs leading to the Study House.

"Hallooo to you, too. We're up here," exclaimed Mirna as Chantal walked to the door to let the men in.

Mirna also walked to the door. She gave Francisco a kiss on the cheek, "I thought the dishes would take a bit longer to clean."

Francisco and Alphonse's faces reddened as they looked at each other and Alphonse grinned as Francisco finally admitted, "Our dear Teresa said she could do a better job cleaning than us men and shooed us out the door. I cannot understand why, but I suspect that when Alphonse picked up a pot scrubbing brush and asked her if we were to scrub the floors, too, is partly the reason."

The others snorted and, with good humor, chastised the men for shirking their duties. After they had dressed in the warm outerwear, hats, and boots that were always stored in the Study House the friends stepped outside. A heavy snow was falling and Mirna, Chantal, and Nonna Maria raised sturdy black umbrellas to ward off insistent flakes. Concealed in the shaft of each umbrella was a long, sharp, deadly rapier blade. Additionally, all the men held loaded muskets and sheathed cutlasses to deal with any hungry animals, enterprising highway men or other interlopers on the broad *La Estancia* estate.

Alphonse smiled grimly at Nonna Maria. "Bears have been sighted nearby, Maria. Have you some way of defending yourself from them and intruders when you travel by yourself? If not we can provide you with the means to fight back."

Nonna Maria grasped the side of her cloak and pulled the edge back, revealing a brace of small pistols and a twenty-inch Roman short sword sheathed in its intricately decorated scabbard, 'The Sword that Conquered the World'. Good enough for a Roman centurion – good enough for me. One of three that have been in my family for sixteen generations. Papa taught all his children how to protect themselves. When I stop traveling I will give it to my nephew, to teach his children. Now, I've other ways to reach out and touch my opponent from further away, as well. I might be an old woman, but I am not a *foolish* old woman."

Alphonse kissed her on the cheek and said, "I say, Maria, I *knew* I liked you. Ever used them?"

Nonna Maria crossed herself. "No, I haven't been in any circumstances that required them being revealed. I listen to my God-given intuition and He has protected me well."

The group then moved onto the flagstone leading down a steep path toward what seemed to be an ordinary group of structures. At the first, an angel standing next to the door waved to Alphonse, then went inside. The way was far and wind had risen by halfway along the path. Snow was falling harder, with countless numbers of large white flakes piling up on the ground. The accumulation measured over a half dozen inches and the leaden sky promised more. The grounds were quickly being transformed into a winter wonderland.

Francisco noticed Alphonse walking with his mouth open and tongue out in the air. He said to Alphonse, "Good thing there aren't any flies this time of year, *amigo*."

Embarrassed, Alphonse chuckled. "There is an old saying in my family: 'The first snowflake of the year is always the tastiest.' I was simply honoring an old tradition."

As the group neared the first growing-house, Nonna Maria commented that all the growing-houses at *La Estancia* had steeply tilted roofs and opaque windows. She then asked why the glass was not clear like so many others she had seen.

Chantal answered, "We diffuse the sunlight with these special windows, Nonna Maria. We can get very even lighting from the sun with no areas that are hotter or colder than others. The roof line is steep so we can prevent most snow accumulation. What little snow sticks usually melts from the temperature below and we collect that water for the plants."

She opened the door and the group followed her into a small glass room with another door on the other side.

Mirna carefully closed the door to the outside and she, Chantal, Francisco, and Alphonse examined the floor, walls, and ceiling before Chantal opened the other door leading inside.

When questioned by Prince Samuel, Francisco replied, "We try to keep the temperature inside even and pests outside. We do a lot of work with selective pollen seeding; that is, moving the pollen into the part of the flowering plants creates new plants. Even one stray worker bee or insect or animal can contaminate a large number of plants. Even though the temperature is low, we always make a habit of looking for intruders."

The group moved into the growing-house and the princes at once noticed that the temperature had risen, creating a pleasant, dry atmosphere in the long rectangular room. The ceiling was low and appeared to be heavily insulated, but there were seams and an odd mechanism on the wall.

Chantal pointed at the mechanism and seams in the ceiling and said, "Alphonse designed the ceiling to open and allow light to enter and close to retain the heat. There is a glass outer roof on top of the ceiling. "

The group doffed their coats and hats.

Mirna said, "Here is where we are working to create vegetables that grow in less than ideal conditions, and are nourishing, but need very little water."

Prince Solomon said, "Any success?"

Alphonse chuckled and said, "Many of the vegetables from last night's dinner were grown here, my friend. Most of the citrus, too."

The two princes exchanged glances. Prince Solomon nodded at Prince Samuel, who turned back to Mirna and Chantal.

Prince Samuel said, "The people of my country are very impressed with the miracle of your beautiful winter roses. Unlike Tierary, the interior of my country is arid and always hot. Fortunately, the coastal areas are blessed with mild, tropical weather and most of our populace lives there."

"As future king of Deltanos and on behalf of my citizens, I have a proposition for you. Could you develop a rose that blooms in the Deltanosian interior as the Torrie does in winter? And a blooming, climbing vine and a low shrub for us that flourish with very little water? Perhaps a fast growing conifer? You would be well compensated indeed."

All eyes of the group were now on Mirna and Chantal.

Mirna extended a hand toward the last group of growing-houses and Chantal said with an enigmatic smile, "Do you ask the impossible, Prince Samuel of Deltanos? How can such wonders be developed? Well, do not be dismayed. Perhaps after many years of development, we may have some success. We will talk about such things later. But for now, shall we visit the last growing- house on the end?"

The seven put their coats and hats back on in the antechamber, exited the growing-house and soon were at their destination.

En route, Alphonse again honored his ancestors as the quiet snow continued to drop from the sky.

The windows on the last growing house were different from the others, and there was no snow on the gentle, curving roof or on the immediate grounds around the building.

"This building is much larger than the others. The roof is different and the windows are dark. That's odd. You cannot see inside. Why is that?" questioned Nonna Maria.

"Patience, Nonna Maria." was Mirna's reply.

The windows of the antechamber were the same dark materials as the windows on the outside.

As soon as the group closed the outer door and searched for intruders, Mirna opened the inner door; the princes gasped with astonishment. Waves of heat enveloped the group and they were quick to shed their outerwear.

The princes stepped into the structure and found themselves standing on a narrow wooden platform elevated several inches above a lush, vegetated but obviously arid desert landscape. Succulent green plants flourished in the dry conditions. Scattered here and there among the cacti were chest high shrubs bearing juicy red berries; off to the left was a climbing vine that entwined itself around and among the limbs of mesquite trees, cacti, and a tall rock formation. The vine's blossoms, longer than a tall man's arm, were delicately colored in a variety of shades and hues. As the group watched, several of the petals changed color, from a gentle peach to a vivid, dusky red, then shifted to a sweet shade of royal blue.

After several speechless moments, the royals and Nonna Maria turned to face Mirna and Chantal.

Chantal said, "The petals somehow stay the same color when picked, but when they fall off by themselves, they change color to deep mahogany. Regardless of how, once they are away from the plant, the petals decay quickly. However, if one were to immerse them in a weak vinegar solution, they assume a tough, leather-like consistency. They last for a long time."

With a small motion of her hand, Chantal gestured to the left and continued, "Hot Torries are around the bend."

Nonna Maria took an embroidered bandanna from her purse, mopped her brow, and spoke rapidly in Tuscan, French, and Spanish.

Switching back to English, she muttered, "And I thought the light-roses in the passageway were exceptional. *These* plants are the most amazing things I have seen in all my years. And goodness, the temperature is hot in here. How do you make conditions like summer in the desert when snow is falling outside?"

Mirna grinned. "Thank you, Nonna Maria. Yes, it's hot because we needed to simulate conditions in the desert. We heat the growing house with our slow-burning trees."

Turning to the men, Mirna continued, "As you can see, we already have the plants you want, Prince Samuel. Many others, too. You see, in order to understand how Torries could bloom in the coldest of winter, we needed to understand why some plants like the cactus thrive in the hottest of summer. So, we traveled to the African Sahara Desert and studied how desert plants exist in extreme conditions. Then, in our growing-houses, we developed a heat resistant species of rose, reversed the process and developed a rose that grows and blooms in frigid conditions. To make sure we understood the process, we then developed a low, leafy shrub and a climbing vine along with several other plants. The shrub has tasty and nutritious fruit as well. The Lord gave us an unexpected bonus with the vine, too."

"Not only are the flowers beautiful but when treated their large petals are tough enough to serve as shoe leather. The chief of our stables and captain of our carriage, Penn the Scot, fashions his boots, saddles, tack and other leather needs for the horses and carriages from them. Andrew named the low shrubs '*Chanisó*' after his guardian angel and the climbing vine *Chasaloté* after another angel whom he says plays the most beautiful music to the Lord. Come, there's more to see around the bend in the walk."

Hearing this, Alphonse's pulse quickened. He said as casually as he could to Francisco, "I say, Andrew is familiar with angels, old chap?"

Francisco nodded. "So he says, *amigo*. He is an innocent child and is not far removed from the Lord. Perhaps."

With Nonna Maria and the princes in tow, Mirna and Chantal led the group further along the elevated wooden path.

Prince Samuel stopped, pointed at a small, nondescript plant a few feet away from the path and exclaimed, "There. That's a Hot Torrie, right? The petals and leaves look just like the plants in your courtyard."

Chantal replied, "Good observation, Samuel. Yes, that's an immature plant. We shall see both young and mature plants as we continue this way."

As the group crested a small rise and rounded a large rock formation. Ahead were several large bushes like the smaller one at the base of the hill. On each bush were a mixture of rose buds and blossoms in several different colors and sizes. As a slight breeze caused each plant to bob, each rose petal shimmered with iridescence. A marvelous rose-scented fragrance wafted toward the group.

Prince Solomon laughed with glee, and, unable to contain his joy, danced a little dance. He said again and again merrily, "Hot Torries. Hot Torries. How fabulous. How beautiful. How did you do know? I knew you could."

Prince Solomon stood with a bemused look on his face.

A grinning Alphonse said to Prince Solomon, "I say, old chap, don't get too carried away with joy."

Finally, Prince Solomon said in a voice choked with emotion, "This is a dream come true. The wastelands of our country can be beautiful at last."

Francisco said, "Yes, but not only beautiful, *amigo*, but profitable as well. With the proceeds from the cultivation of the leather blossoms of the *Lotés* and the fruit of the '*Nisos*, just think of the poverty and suffering that can be eased. And not just in your country. New uses will be found for the 'Loté blossoms. There will be whole new industries created. Citizens can work their way out of poverty and not be beholden to the government for assistance. Your region and indeed that whole part of the world can experience an economic renaissance similar to the one in Europe now."

Prince Samuel continued the thought, "Yes, Francisco, and a cultural renaissance as well. As our citizens have their material needs met, they will have more ability to focus on higher needs like literature, and art, and music. A true renaissance, indeed."

Mirna said, "There is a bit of concern, however. We fear that the Hot Torries, *Chañisós* and *Chasalotés* will too drastically change the ecological balance of your country because the plants will slowly replenish the soil with their life cycle. Other plants that may tolerate the heat but needed better nutrients will start to grow and so on."

Chantal said, "Slowly, the region will change. Perhaps the weather as well. We have tried to remedy this by designing the '*Lotés* and Hot Torries to grow rapidly and then die in one season rather than taking several years to mature. They are a good source of fuel and materials for shelter too."

Prince Samuel said, "But changing the unusable land in our country to usable *is* a worthy endeavor. Our country is lush and tropical near the coasts but the vast interior is barren and uninhabitable. Nothing grows there. Nothing lives there. Not even insects."

Prince Solomon said out loud but to himself, "Except for the 'Lost Ones'."

"Lost Ones, Solomon? You believe that old myth about a tribe of ancients and a hidden civilization in the interior of Deltanos? I thought that was just legend." Alphonse scratched his nose. "But most often, myth emerges from some long ago point of fact."

Samuel broke in, "Solomon may believe that but I do not, Alphonse. Surely they would have been discovered by now."

Francisco laughed. "An adventure yet to happen, *amigos*. We must visit someday and mount an expedition to find them. Who knows, perhaps Andrew himself will make the discovery."

Mirna said, "Well, Samuel, just between us, if one were to prune the lowest branches of the plants in their first few weeks of growth, they would last several years. Maybe longer. Their seeds would then produce saplings that would grow over a much longer period of time. For example, these Hot Torries in front of us are over three years old."

Chantal walked over to where several *Chanisó* shrubs were growing and returned with an apron pocket full of large, plum-sized red berries. Passing them around to the group, she seemed pleased by the amazed looks on Nonna Maria and the two princes' faces when they tasted the fruit.

Nonna Maria looked at the fruit in her hand. "*Mama mia.* What marvelous flavors these have. Tart, yet sweet. They remind me of peaches and raspberries and oranges and lemons mixed together. Oh, to have these back in Tuscany for our pastries, jellies, and jams. You must give me some to take back to the Angel School. I will make jams and jellies for the children. They would love such a treat."

Mirna smiled. "Of course, Nonna Maria. Take all you wish, but you must send us some of the jam you make when Andrew returns home on the weekends."

Nonna Maria nodded her assent. "Of course."

With a distant look on his face, Prince Samuel said, "The 'Niso berries could become a lucrative export product if we could grow enough. The *'Lotés*, why, they have the potential to be a marvelous export product too."

Francisco grinned. "Always thinking ahead. Unfortunately, the 'Nisos stay fresh but a short time after they ripen and so we have difficulty shipping them far without taking expensive special precautions, using current shipping techniques."

With a twinkle in his eye, Prince Solomon said, "I see where this thought will lead." He continued, "But that is with *current*, conventional shipping techniques. Our new company can overcome this problem, and in a cost-effective way. Good Heavens. We will earn more profit than we will know what to do with."

Prince Solomon paused as if to consider his thoughts.

He said, "Friends, I propose that we keep but a small portion for ourselves and utilize the rest to overcome poverty, promoting education, and doing the Lord's work. And not just in Deltanos or Tierary, but worldwide."

Alphonse and Francisco said almost as one, "That is what we had in mind as well."

Prince Samuel stood before the ladies. "You truly amaze me with your ingenuity. As I said before, we would like to purchase the Hot Torries and certainly the other plants, too. Although our country is poor, we will pay you whatever you wish for such treasures."

Chantal walked toward and stood next to Alphonse. Mirna did the same with Francisco. The men put their arms around their wives. The four then turned and faced Nonna Maria and the two princes.

Mirna said gently, "Prince Samuel, Prince Solomon, the Hot Torrie Rose plants, the *Chasalotés* and *Chañisós* are not for sale. You see, they are easy to grow but only in arid wastelands quite similar to your native country. With the heartfelt approval of Snorffleham Palace and on behalf of the citizens of Tierary, please accept them as a gift from our country to yours."

Chantal added, "And, you may have the *Chanisó* shrub and *Chasaloté* climbing vine as well. Again, as our gift. We developed them for Deltanos and they will grow nowhere else. May our countries always be close friends and allies."

Overwhelmed at their generosity, the men briefly hugged Mirna and Chantal, then turned and hugged Francisco and Alphonse.

Although speechless at first, Prince Samuel soon regained his wits. Clearing his throat he said, "On behalf of my father the king, and the royal court in Soncidros, I accept your generosity. I am certain our countries will be the warmest of friends for many, many generations. Thank you. My heart is soaring with the highest falcons."

Nonna Maria smiled and said, "You know, Prince Samuel, I have a feeling that you will grow into a fine and benevolent king."

Solomon echoed his cousin. "And my heart is walking on clouds as well, Nonna Maria." Turning to the two couples, he said, "Thank you, old friends. The Lord has blessed us again. Praise be to the Lord."

Nonna Maria said, "I believe a deepening friendship between Tierary and Deltanos has been born at this moment. We should pray and thank the Lord for His giving Mirna and Chantal the knowledge to develop such miracles and the wisdom of how to share these treasures."

The group murmured their assent and the old schoolteacher led the group in a brief but heartfelt prayer of thanksgiving and praise. As the prayer ended, Alphonse said with a chuckle, "Jolly good show. But now let us enjoy a change of scenery. This growing-house is hot as a hearth, and I'm roasting. Let us take our leave and be on our way. Onward to *Mañana* Hill."

Chapter Seventeen
Preparations

With Solomon, Samuel and Nonna Maria still dazzled at the wonders behind them, the group stepped back into the antechamber for a few minutes to prepare themselves for the soon-to-come drastic temperature change.

Francisco checked to see if the others were ready, then cracked the outer door. The frigid wind swirled into the small chamber, bringing along a flurry of snowflakes, which quickly melted to form a puddle on the floor.

Alphonse was the last person out. "Ah, yes, that's the climate I love so much. I say, the snow is now up to my ankles. Perfect," said Alphonse, taking a deep breath as he stepped back onto the now hidden flagstone path. Already his hat was collecting a white, wintry coating. Francisco laughed and slapped Alphonse on his shoulder. He said, "*Amigo*, I believe that you would be happy in a blinding snowstorm at the top of the world."

Alphonse grinned and said, "Yes, but only in mid-winter. The Northern Lights are quite a sight to see."

Nonna Maria stopped and said, "The dancing fire in the sky? The ancient Norse thought the Northern Lights was light being released from glaciers. You have been to the top of the world and seen the fire in the sky? I have always wanted to see them. What do they look like?"

Alphonse replied, "Well, Nonna Maria, one winter many years ago, Chantal and I were guests of the Norwegian Royal Confectionery and visited their northernmost operation in Tannerholm." He paused and reminisced, "They raise the oddest livestock there – No, not the top of the world but certainly we could see it from there." He smiled. "I always love that old joke. Anyway, we experienced an all-day night and enjoyed the light spectacle several times."

Nonna Maria broke in, "All-day night? And what do they look like?"

Alphonse continued, "As you know, during the winter in the northern climes, darkness rules the day for most of the time. That's when you see them. They look like thick ribbons or even curtains of glowing light that start in the far north and then travel toward you; curling, swirling, shimmering, dancing, and undulating all across the sky overhead. Sometimes the color is golden, sometimes red, and other times blue or green. The lights last from a few minutes to several hours. I say, they are quite beautiful, actually."

Prince Samuel said, "Do they make any noise? Can you touch them?"

Alphonse said, "No, they are high up in the sky, completely silent. Yet one could maybe imagine a virtuoso violinist accompanied by a master concert cellist performing a musical score that would be a perfect match."

After a moment's reflection, he added, "But no, perhaps only angels of the Lord could play that well."

Chantal broke in, "Yes, Samuel, they are truly an impressive and inspiring sight. You should see them before you become king."

Prince Samuel stopped and turned to look back toward the growing-house containing the Hot Torries, *Chañisós* and *Chasalotés*. He stood still for a long moment and snowflakes began nesting in his knit cap. Finally, he said, "Yes, I think that I will someday; however, I cannot think that there's much that would impress me more than your marvelous accomplishments in those buildings."

Underneath her umbrella, Mirna brushed back an errant lock of graying hair. She kissed his forehead, and said, "You are kind indeed, Samuel, but you are young and the world is full of wonders yet unseen."

With that, the group returned to the Study House. As boots were being stomped and coats shaken to remove excess snow, plans were made for the afternoon.

Francisco announced, "Here is what we propose for the rest of the day: Let us meet in the foyer of the main house, say, in *un hora*, one hour? Bueno. Penn the Scot will drive us to *Manaña* Hill in 'Squeaky', our trusty sleigh. We shall tackle the Hill and then warm ourselves afterwards with dinner in *La Casita*, our home at the base. We shall spend the night there and perhaps another, then return in the late afternoon tomorrow or the following day. Or whenever we decide, for there is much beauty surrounding *La Casita*. Crestina and her sister Angeline will join us there by dinner time tonight as well."

Alphonse reminded Francisco, "Have you made arrangements for a second sleigh to take us back to the top of the Hill after we have ridden down? Otherwise we will be racing Penn down the mountain all day. Remember last time?"

Francisco laughed and said, "*Sí, amigo. Yo requerdo*. I remember. We won every race. What a day that was. But I think Penn received great enjoyment from racing us on our fast toboggans too. No, my friend, I have not forgotten. Today, as usual, we will have two sleighs and an additional one as well. Penn has hired his comrade, Ayres the shopkeeper, to assist."

Prince Solomon stepped forward. "We do not have appropriate clothing for romping in the snow, my friend. Do you have something that will fit us?"

Francisco said, "You will find what you each need in one of the closets in the Guest House, *amigo*. And in *La Casita*, too."

Turning to Nonna Maria and Chantal, Mirna said, "Nonna Maria, even though you are not planning on joining us on the toboggan, you should use the garments in your room as well. Sometimes the weather gets colder than we plan for. Chantal, as you know, there are suitable clothes for you and Alphonse in the closet in your room."

Chantal murmured her thanks and Nonna Maria replied, "Thank you. And we should all shall check on Sophie before we leave."

The group then dispersed to prepare for an afternoon spent out of doors.

After about an hour had passed, Alphonse and Chantal met the others in the foyer.

Penn the Scot, clad in a heavy, gray, woolen greatcoat, black bowler hat and red-and-white-striped scarf wrapped around his thick neck, had hitched his team of eight horses to Squeaky, the antique iron and wood, three-row sleigh. Penn had driven around to the front of the Great House and was ready to depart. Shiny brass and nickel sleigh bells, each the size of Andrew's fist hung on bright red and green ribbons from the back of the black sleigh and the horses' harnesses. Attached to the rear of the sleigh by tandem 'Loté' fiber ropes were three sleek toboggans affectionately named *La Rikkita de las Rosas*, *Rebecca del Cielo*, and Princess Domani, their names fancily painted in glitter on their highly polished curved wooden fronts.

The snowfall had eased, although here and there scattered flakes still made their way to join their fellows already on the ground. To Alphonse's practiced eye, more snow was on the way.

Andrew, all bundled up in a colorful wrap that reminded Alphonse of a large cocoon, was seated in his usual place on Penn's lap. Prince Samuel, clad like the other men, in a warm waistcoat, earmuffs, stocking cap and heavy black woolen trousers, sat perched next to the two on the driver's seat.

Penn was engaged in lively conversation with Francisco and *Prince* Samuel.

Prince Samuel said, "I have heard much about your drives to the Angel School, Mister Penn. If the others are so inclined, can we have such a drive today?"

Penn replied, "Aye, Prince Samuel. That can be arranged, with the approval of *Don* Francisco and the others. This wee lad, might I correct myself and say wee but *growing* lad, on my lap, I believe, will concur."

A single honk signaled Andrew's agreement and everyone laughed.

Francisco grinned, "Then you have my approval as well, *amigo*. Take us on a thrilling ride."

On the next row directly behind Penn and the others were Prince Solomon, Francisco and Mirna. After exchanging greetings, Alphonse and Chantal climbed up onto the sleigh and joined Nonna Maria on the back row. Chantal inquired about Sophie and Nonna Maria reported that she was awake but still feverish and would benefit from bed rest. "She should be fine when we return," said Nonna Maria as Alphonse stood to urge Penn to make a rapid start.

"The last row of the sleigh gets the most motion as we ride. My favorite place to sit," exclaimed Alphonse to Nonna Maria, who nervously smiled back. Excitement tinged the cold, crisp air, and the team of horses snorted and pawed the ground, impatient to be on their way.

"Here you are, your own blanket just for the two of you," said Mirna as she handed a heavy, folded woolen cover to Alphonse and Chantal. "And one for you, Nonna Maria." The bright bands of green, blue, and red on the fabric were inlaid with an intricate, ornate pattern. The others were already similarly bundled up against the cold.

Ill-meaning intruders accosting the group would be in for an unpleasant surprise as each passenger had two pistols, a rifle, and other weapons in their possession.

Mirna noticed Alphonse and Chantal examining the blanket and remarked, "We have had these covers in the family for many generations. Somehow, they stand the ravages of time and weather, and so we keep using them."

Alphonse replied, "Do the patterns have any significance, Mirna? They seem to be like pieces of a giant puzzle. How many do you have?"

"We have nine, and you may have something there. Sometime we should match up each one with the corresponding sides of the others and see what the puzzle makes."

"Yes. We love a puzzle," agreed Alphonse as he unfolded the cover and placed the wrap over Chantal and himself. The two snuggled closer together.

With a gleam in his eye, Penn looked backwards from his perch and watched as the royals and Nonna Maria climbed up onto the sleigh. Finally, confident that the last of his passengers was safely aboard, he called out in a loud voice in his thick Scottish brogue, "Are ye ready, *Don* Francisco?"

"Ready, Mister Penn," came his reply.

"Aye. Are we ready? Marvelous." Looking down at the excited youth on his lap, the Scot said in a commanding voice that grew in volume as he spoke. "Andrew, me lad, do ye wish to fly today? Tell me, laddie, do ye want to fly as an eagle-falcon today? Yes? Then toot yer brass horn, mon. Honk yer horn for all it's worth and let the world know that it's me lad Andrew's time to go."

Rapid, excited honking came from the front of the sleigh as Andrew giggled.

Nonna Maria, a tight, apprehensive smile on her weathered face, muttered a muffled, *'Mama Mia'* under her woolen scarf.

Prince Solomon's leather gloved hands tightened on the side rail. Mirna and Chantal laughed excitedly as Francisco called out, "Hang on folks. Here we go." Penn sent the horsewhip in motion, whistling twice high above his head and then suddenly flashed toward the lead horse. The air was pierced with the sound of a loud *crack*. The startled team of horses snorted and lunged ahead. In an instant the sleigh shot forward, its iron runners breaking the frozen bond that had stuck the sled to the snow. Soon the sled was gliding over fresh powder.

The Scot roared, "Onward. Onward through the forest, Andrew me lad. Onward through the fields and over the hills and dales. Toot yer horn Andrew me lad, for all you're worth. We're

FREE. Free as a falcon. Free as an eagle. Freedom awaits. Fast-

er, laddie, faster still. Onward, man, to *Mañana* Hill. "

Chapter Eighteen
Squeaky

Effortlessly, the powerful team of horses pulled Squeaky out the main gate, down a slight hill and across the covered bridge over Beaver Creek. The sleigh passed by snow-laden evergreens passed on each side in a breathtaking blur of winter beauty.

The snow-covered road took a sudden dogleg to the right and for a moment the occupants felt themselves pressed hard against the sleigh slowed and made its way through a snow drift. Penn guided the team of horses around a series of bends in the road and up a long and gradual rise.

Andrew's honking horn and the merry ching-ching sound of the sleigh bells eased Nonna Maria's apprehension and soon she told the others that she was enjoying the ride.

The group was startled by Prince Samuel's excited shout, "LOOK." Pointing to the left side of the road, he said sheepishly, "Torrie Roses." He pointed to the right. "There, too. And there. Hundreds of them. How beautiful." Eyes sparkling, he turned back to a smiling Solomon and said, "Solomon, we will soon be saying this about the interior of Deltanos, too."

His face beaming, Prince Solomon replied, "Indeed we will, my good Samuel."

Everybody added their congratulations again and Chantal said, "All in good time, Samuel. We must get your Hot Torries to Deltanos and plant them first."

Happiness and excitement again filled the air.

The team of horses soon slowed to a brisk clip and soon three hours had passed with the wonders of winter flashing by. The road maintained a gradual rise in elevation, with fields and forests alternating on both sides.

The sleigh entered a forested area heavy with huge oak, elm and walnut trees. Penn the Scot announced that they would soon be stopping at a small inn for a brief rest for the horses.

Alphonse remarked, "Indeed, my dear Penn, your timing is perfect. Like your splendid horses, we humans need to warm our old bones as well." The group stirred restlessly and after a few more miles Penn guided Squeaky into a clearing and stopped in front of a delightful, quaint cottage and inn. As soon as the sleigh was empty, he drove it around back to tend to the horses' needs.

Entering through the front door, the group was greeted by the owners and urged to remove their outer garments and make themselves comfortable. Coffee, tea, and a light meal were served. The owners were old acquaintances of Francisco and Mirna and the four spent several minutes catching up on events in each other's lives.

The stone fireplace in the middle of the room received the addition of several medium and one large log and soon was providing warmth and light for the entire dining area.

Prominent in the large room was a massive, stuffed moose head sporting antlers almost as wide as the wall it was hanging from. The trophy elicited several comments from the two princes, and the innkeeper told the two that the mountain range was teeming with wildlife, ranging from the tiny chipmunk squirrel to the mighty forest bear, although there hadn't been a bear sighting in a year.

The innkeeper explained that trapping or hunting animals that the hunter was not going to use for food or clothing, was strictly forbidden. Samuel and Solomon nodded, adding that this sensible policy was law in their land also, and that adults were required to maintain their own rifles, pistols and swords to assist the military in case of need. The group spent several minutes stretching and warming themselves in the radiant heat.

The inn was comfortable and the conversation lively, but all too soon, Penn the Scot entered the front door and announced that it was time to go.

This time the horses started without the need of the whip, as if the animals knew that they would soon be at their destination. As the sleigh rounded a sharp bend in the road flanked by tall evergreens on both sides, tiny snowflakes started falling again, riding a cold and rising wind.

Alphonse started humming a bright and joyous worship song. Francisco joined in, as did Prince Samuel and Prince Solomon. Humming turned into song and Penn the Scot's thick brogue added a unique flavor to the men's voices. Nonna Maria accompanied Chantal and Mirna in the chorus. As their voices praising God rose in unison, everyone was startled to hear Andrew join the singing, also praising God in a sweet, pure voice.

The adult's voices trailed off in wonderment and Penn allowed the sleigh to come to a gradual stop as Andrew continued singing. When he finished, a stunned silence had enveloped the sleigh. Even the birds of the forest were still.

Mirna scrambled down from the sleigh and gathered her son from Penn. For a long time she sat in the middle of the snowy road, rocking the happy boy in her arms, unable to stop her sobbing. "Andrew, Andrew, Andrew." The youth hugged her tightly, "Momma. Momma. Momma. I love you so."

As tears of joy streamed down his face, a speechless Francisco spread his strong but gentle arms around the pair as one by one the others climbed down from the sleigh and held the happy family.

With shining eyes, Andrew looked up at his parents, smiled his lopsided grin and said in a clear voice, "Hi Momma. Hi Papa. I love you."

Mirna said, "Andrew, you can sing. You can speak. Andrew, my beloved son. You can sing. Praise God. Thank you Lord for this beautiful gift."

Tears of rejoicing streamed down Alphonse's face and fell on his coat. He said jubilantly, "Our Sing Song Child will be truly able to sing songs with us. Praise God for this gift."

Andrew smiled. "Momma, I am tired." He then fell into a deep sleep.

Nonna Maria bent over the inert boy and noticed for the first time the coarsening hairs on his upper lip. He's growing up quickly, she thought. She lifted his eyelids, peered into his sleeping eyes, listened to his breathing and said a short prayer. When she lifted her head, tears of relief shone in her eyes. Looking at Francisco and Mirna, she smiled and said, "This youngster has had quite a day. Andrew should sleep for a while and then wake up. He may or may not recall what just happened and we should treat him as if nothing has happened at all."

She stood, looked up at the others and continued, "I have prayed for this to happen, as have we all. I know from past conversations that you, Francisco and you, Mirna, have long thought that someday Andrew could be capable of normal speech. He seemed to be right on the verge so many times. Today was that day. God does miracles, does He not?"

"And so a miracle was worked here in our presence. The Lord has smiled on this child. Do not be alarmed if when he wakes up, for many weeks or perhaps even half a year he cannot speak well again. Something in his head just started working the right way for the first time in Andrew's life but he may not remember how to again for a while. And further proof of God's goodness is that Angeline is coming to be his teacher. Cases like this are her area of expertise. Andrew's progress will certainly quicken with her tutelage. Praise God." Francisco said in his deep voice, "Let us give Him thanks for this miracle," and led the others in a brief yet deeply heartfelt prayer. The group climbed back into the sleigh, with Prince Solomon joining Prince Samuel and Penn the Scot in the front seat. Francisco held his wife and son, and the two sat close together in the middle seat, holding the still sleeping Andrew on their laps.

Just as Penn was to set the team of horses into motion, the cheery, melodious sound of sleigh bells and horses' hooves came from behind the sleigh. Penn had the horses move Squeaky forward and over to the side a bit so the other sleigh could pass on the left. The second sleigh drew abeam and stopped. Waving from the rear seat were Crestina and her sister Angeline. In the front seat sat Penn's comrades-in-arms Ayres, the shopkeeper, and Peel the carriage driver. In the back seat was a large, ornately decorated box.

There was a brief, excited exchange of greetings as Mirna, Chantal, and Nonna Maria told Crestina and Angeline what had just happened. Angeline questioned Mirna about

Andrew's choice of words and pronunciation; Peel helped her climb down from the sleigh and the group waited quietly as she examined the sleeping youth.

Satisfied, Angeline looked up, smiled sweetly and said in a gentle, melodic French accent, "He is well, this boy. Andrew shall sleep but a little more and wake to find that his little world is now big with possibility. We have much hard work to do, but clearly a good thing has happened this day."

She deferred further speculation until she could interact with Andrew, and the unanimous decision was made to head directly to *La Casita* at the base of *Manaña* Hill instead of going directly to the runs at the top of the hill.

At once the two sleighs were on their way. After a few minutes, Alphonse pointed out a familiar landmark to Nonna Maria and said, "There's Montoya Rock. The road forks here. To the left and up a bit is the *Hill* to the right; and down is La Casita. We should be there shortly."

Chapter Nineteen
La Casita

As the two sleighs continued down the road, the pine forest thinned and soon the sleighs emerged into a valley. On the right was an old but well-kept two-story log mansion encircled by a wide covered porch. Further to the left and down was a forty-acre, ice-covered lake with a thickly forested island in the middle. A herd of elk melted into the island's trees just as they approached. Here and there around the structure and scattered throughout the landscape, hundreds of bud-tipped Torrie Roses lent their vibrant green beauty to the wintry wonderland.

Francisco handed the still-sleeping Andrew out of the sleigh to Penn, who turned and gently carried him into the house. Prince Samuel brought the large box from the back seat and set it on the floor near the door. Ayres and Peel quickly built a warming fire in the fireplace and one in the stove for tea. Angeline had Penn lay the sleeping boy on a leather couch and removed his warm outerwear and boots. Covering him with a light but comfortable duvet, she examined Andrew once again and turned to the others.

Angeline said gently, "Andrew will be sleeping for another hour, yet. We must make the excitement less when he wakes. There is little that can be done for him now, and I would like to interact with him in quiet then. *Doña* Mirna, Chantal, Crestina and Nonna Maria shall stay with me. The rest must go to enjoy the snow."

Francisco protested that he, too, wanted to stay with his son, only to be interrupted by kind but firm words from Mirna. "Angeline is right, Francisco. And you are to take the others down the Hill. Be my eyes and tell me how the gentlemen handle the ride." She gave him a light kiss on the lips and whispered something in his ear. Francisco's eyes grew wide and he allowed himself the smallest of smiles. He held her close and whispered something back into Mirna's ear, then watched as she blushed and smiled back, eyes shining.

Francisco relented after several more minutes of assurances that Andrew would receive the best of care. He winked at Mirna and said, "Then we shall return with tales of the prince's debut. I will make their introduction to *Manaña* Hill a memorable one."

Angeline said, "Today belongs to Andrew, but maybe we can ride your wooden devices down the hill tomorrow. Do you have some head protectors to stop you from injury? This is my area of knowledge, and many injuries can be prevented by simply using common sense and protective gear. The thicker the padding between one's skull and whatever it hits the better."

Alphonse grinned and said, "I say, my dear Angeline, we are in no danger on the Hill. Whatever could happen?"

Chantal stepped forward, "Alphonse, please wear your new helmet. You know the Hill can be treacherous, and you must recall your accident of two nights past."

Alphonse softened. "I will, my dear. I promise."

Nonna Maria announced, "I shall go with the men. Andrew is in good hands here and someone must take care of those going. Besides, the cold air is making me feel young again. Who knows, I may even ride one of those 'wooden devices'."

Everyone laughed and said farewell. Soon the cabin was quiet, with only the crackling logs to interrupt the silence.

Angeline and Crestina made themselves busy by lighting the main room's oil lamps, which cast a warm, yellow glow over the interior. When their task was finished, they returned and joined Mirna and Chantal.

The ladies sat on the comfortable chairs flanking the fireplace, sofa and the sleeping Andrew. Mirna said, "Do you think Alphonse will wear his helmet, Chantal? Francisco never does."

Chantal assured her, "Yes, of course he will, Mirna. In the beginning. But you know how he is; Alphonse has such a big heart for children that he will see a child without one and give them his. We have to buy new ones each year. But this year should be different."

Mirna gave Chantal a quizzical look and said," How so?"

A twinkle in her eye, Chantal said, "I had a special helmet made for Alphonse for his birthday. Extra thick padding, custom fit and with his choice of colors and a sentimental inscription on the inside. Maybe he will think twice about giving it away."

Chantal smiled and looked at Mirna, "We have done all that we can. Now it's time to do what we must: pray and give them to the Lord."

Crestina and Angeline returned and sat down on the sofa. Mirna bowed her head and led the four in a brief prayer for

Andrew, protection for those on the Hill and for wisdom in dealing with Andrew's recuperation.

When the four had finished praying, Angeline looked at the others and said, "We need to discuss what to tell Andrew when he wakes."

Just then, a high pitched whistling sound drew all eyes toward the kitchen.

Chantal stood and said, "I say, that's the teakettle. I love that cheery sound. Shall we move this discussion into the kitchen and have some tea?"

20

Chapter Twenty
Up To Mañana Hill

The faint sound of the kettle's whistle reached the toboggans as they pulled away from the house in both sleighs. In no time at all, they had turned around and were on their way up the slope toward the summit.

Alphonse, Peel and Prince Samuel rode in the first sleigh driven by Penn; Francisco, Nonna Maria, Prince Solomon, the second, with Ayres at the helm. Soon, the horses had settled into a comfortable pace up the wide, winding road leading to the top.

Several other roads intersected theirs, and in the first sleigh, Prince Samuel pointed to tracks in the snow in front of them and said, "We will not be alone."

Alphonse responded, "No, Samuel, Mañana Hill is a popular sledding and tobogganing destination for this entire area. With the recent snowfall, we should be in great company, especially for the trip back up the Hill to make another run."

Prince Samuel cast a puzzled look at Alphonse, who chuckled and explained, "As we make our run down the hill on our toboggans, both sleighs will be in constant use. One of the sleighs will be coming up the hill carrying some of the others who were faster than the others, the other sleigh will be going down the hill after depositing its occupants at the summit.

The road was specifically constructed wider to accommodate two sleighs towing toboggans and sleds abreast at one time. That way we can get in many runs down the hill and not have to walk back up each time."

Samuel said, "Bravo, Alphonse. What clever ideas."

Alphonse beamed and said, "Yes, Samuel, and the idea is quite old. The local population has been enjoying this tradition for centuries. We will be sharing our sleigh with others and perhaps we may ride in a stranger's sleigh as well. And tradition also holds that the owner of the sleighs bring one more driver than needed to allow the other two drivers to take turns resting and enjoying *Manaña* Hill as well. Another tradition is just before the last run of the day, as the sun is setting, we gather our group and anyone nearby and enjoy some confections and have hot cocoa. We should all be tired by then; the break and the sweets will give us a boost of energy. Now let me instruct you in the steering of the toboggan..."

In the other sleigh, Francisco and the others were having much the same conversation. Francisco said to Prince Solomon, "We have three toboggans and six riders. We were to have three or four riders per toboggan, but our number will do. In fact, *amigo*, we will go faster with the lighter load, but will have less control over the toboggan. We must be that much more careful. Generally, the person in the front will do the steering, and I wish to match up an experienced rider with a not so experienced one."

Nonna Maria broke in with a laugh, "Yes, Francisco, an experienced rider with me as well. I haven't ridden since I was a child, and I am now a few years past my childhood." Francisco agreed. "In the beginning, Solomon, I think that you and I will ride the graceful Rikkita, Alphonse and Nonna Maria will ride the gentle Domani, and Peel and Samuel will ride the delicate Rebecca."

Nonna Maria said, "Francisco, you talk about each toboggan as if they have their own personalities."

Francisco said, "Actually, they do, Nonna Maria. *Rikkita de las Rosas* is quite a lady – gracefully, sweetly countenanced yet somehow attracted to our beautiful Torrie Roses. Many times riders have found themselves heading straight for patches of Torrie Rose bushes with only the heroic last-minute actions of the helmsman saving the riders from finding out how sharp those thorns really are."

Rebecca del Cielo translates into "Rebecca of the Clouds" and is so named because somehow, when she hits a bump, the beautifully lithe Rebecca seems as if she is actually flying."

Everyone laughed as they considered the absurd notion of a person soaring through the sky like a bird until Ayres said over his shoulder that he, Penn, and Peel were building a winged frame so that they perhaps a person might capture the wind and glide short distances down an embankment or small hill.

Intrigued, the group questioned Ayres closely until finally, Prince Solomon and the others concluded that with intelligent efforts like these, maybe someday people would indeed fly like birds.

Francisco said, "Princess Domani is so named after a much beloved princess who is supposed to have lived long ago. According to legend, Princess Domani became queen and ruled her land with much wisdom, kindness and compassion for her people, but it was as princess that she really made an impact on her country. In fact, Nonna Maria, it was she who started your Angel School, among many other good works for Tierary."

Nonna Maria gasped, "So she really existed, Francisco? Of course. Domani. Princess Domani. Domani the Kind. I thought she was but a legend. Many years ago I found some old, crumbling papers in a small, ancient trunk in the basement when looking for an oil lamp. I thought they were of no consequence, but respected their age and left them undisturbed. It seemed as if they hadn't been touched for many years. I recall correspondence between a young girl and her mother and some other papers that I did not disturb."

Nonna Maria paused to gather her thoughts and then continued, "Now that I think about the chest, I believe that a person named Domani may have signed some of the letters. Could this be the Princess Domani? Mama mia. I feel foolish to have never considered the possibility."

Prince Solomon chuckled and then said seriously, "Nonna Maria, you may have important historical documents in your possession. Like our Royal Court in Soncidros, your Snorffleham Palace is always searching for its history to record, preserve and cherish. You should contact the palace as soon as you go home."

Nonna Maria smiled and said, "Yes, Solomon, I will. Perhaps the papers will shed light on the lost history of Tierary. I have a friend in university who specializes in Tierarian history. I must let him know of this as soon as I get back to the Angel School. This is exciting. I will let you know of their significance."

Francisco agreed. "Yes, Maria, you may have something important. Domani the Kind's rule is to have lasted for many years and is considered to have triggered a renaissance of sorts right after the 'Time of Trouble'. Your letters may shed some light on what actually happened. No one knows."

The group talked about the history of Tierary for several more minutes and then Francisco gently steered the conversation back to the toboggans.

Francisco continued, "If you notice, Domani is slightly wider than both Rikkita and Rebecca and has small railings built into the sides designed to help secure special passengers, like Andrew. Although all our toboggans can accommodate him, Domani is his favorite, and believe it or not, late last year Andrew took this first run all by himself. Penn and I flanked him on our own toboggans, of course, but Andrew was alone on Domani. You should have seen his face. He was so proud."

The road soon came to a gentle, curving intersection. Both drivers had their horses turn left and continue up the hill after making sure there were no other sleighs in their path.

Prince Samuel said, "Here comes another sleigh. We're getting close."

Sure enough, coming down the hill was another sleigh, empty except for the driver. The driver waved a cheery greeting as he passed on the left and after several minutes the road ended, both sleighs emerging into a cleared area most of the way up *Mañana* Hill, already populated by many people and sleighs of all shapes and sizes. A group of small, tidy cabins were on the far side of the clearing, one of which had the universally-recognized bright blue "Fast Help Now" banner hanging in the front window. From a flagpole in front of another cabin flew a large bright green flag. Beyond the cabins continuing up the slope was a wild, heavily forested area which thinned as the elevation increased; the summit itself was barren and rocky.

Prince Samuel said to Alphonse, "Clarify one thing for me, my friend. Is *Mañana* Hill a hill or a mountain? I have been puzzling over this all day."

Alphonse laughed. "Well, my dear fellow, the 'Hill' is actually one of the five mountains that make up the mighty Calvillo mountain range here in Tierary. This particular mountain is nicknamed *Grande Papa – Big Daddy* in English – but we locals refer to this part as *Mañana* Hill, or 'Tomorrow Hill,' because the more advanced runs are so steep and dangerous that you wonder if you will see another *mañana*."

The sleighs parked and everyone got out and stretched. Several people recognized Alphonse, Francisco, Penn, Peel and Ayres, who smiled and waved back.

Chapter Twenty One
For the Joy of the Ride

*T*he three former comrades-in-arms had already untied the toboggans from Squeaky, the sleigh, and had positioned them in the middle of the beginning of the first run on the left.

As the group was making their preparations, the wind picked up in speed and dark, heavy clouds rolled over the highest peaks of *Mañana* Hill. Large snowflakes started falling and the tops of the pine and hardwood trees started to bend with the force of the wind. A sudden, loud crashing sound caused everyone to turn toward the cabins. Farther up the incline, a large tree limb, overloaded from the abundant snowfall earlier in the day, had torn from the trunk of a mighty oak and plummeted to the ground. The worsening weather lasted but a few moments and soon the wind and snow had lessened.

While the group surveyed the scene, the door of one of the cabins opened and two men came out, one holding a bright yellow, red and green flag at his side. The two walked to a flagpole in front of the cabin. After a brief discussion they attached the flag to the rope of flagpole then hoisted the standard into the sky. The flag had a large yellow band in the center, flanked by a small band of green and red on each side.

Prince Solomon turned to Alphonse and asked, "What's the flag for, Alphonse?"

Alphonse replied, "Members of the Board of Entry keep close tabs on weather conditions, Solomon. When, in their experience, a threat to the people using the Hill exists, they raise a pennant corresponding to the degree of danger. A blue ensign signifies no danger. A flag that is mostly green and has smaller yellow and red bands means that there is relatively little danger from avalanches, blizzards and the sort. If you notice, this flag is almost all yellow, with smaller bands of green and red on each end and stands for caution. A red flag tells us that there is an immediate danger; to cease our activities and get down from *Manaña* Hill."

Prince Samuel asked, "So why is the caution flag out?"

Alphonse responded, "Probably because of the heavy clouds and the falling limb we heard before. Where there's one, there will be more, but I think we should be safe." He glanced up the Hill and said, "But we shall have riding weather for only a few more hours. Then we must be off the Hill and on our way to *La Casita*. There seems to be a major storm on the way."

Francisco consulted with Alphonse about his toboggan assignments, and then with both men in agreement, briefed the two princes, Nonna Maria and the three drivers.

Francisco said, "The layouts of the runs down the hill are quite simple; the easy runs are on the left, getting harder the farther right you go. Between each run is an observation lane, constructed for getting to those who, for one reason, or another may need assistance while on the active run. As a general rule, children and novices start on the left because the slope is gentle and there are many places to stop and rest or just enjoy the Hill. That is where we will start as well, gentlemen, because this is your first time here. Nonna Maria, we will start here also, because you have not ridden for many years. As you master the toboggan and build confidence, we will graduate to the runs further right. The runs in the middle and going to the right are faster, and the furthest run on the right is for those who have the courage of a lion. Some have the skill to master the challenge, but few have the courage, and so few try. By the way, our own Alphonse's nickname is Alphonse the Lionhearted."

Sheepishly, Alphonse said, "Francisco, you have the same moniker as well." Turning to face the others, he explained, "When you complete five right-most runs in one year for two consecutive seasons, you are admitted as a full member into the Lionheart Club and the group adds the nickname 'The Lionhearted' to your name. It's all jolly good fun. Penn, Peel and Ayres are judges and members of the Board of Entry as well. We have all been riding for years. In fact, because of last year's late snows, Chantal and Mirna are but one ride away from membership and they can gain entry this season, probably this week if they choose to ride tomorrow or the next few days. Andrew was initiated into the Little Lionheart Club immediately after his solo run."

Prince Samuel stepped forward and said, "This Lionheart Club is a worthy goal. One day perhaps I shall be a member too."

Nonna Maria said, "A worthy goal indeed. I cannot recall, Samuel, do you have a mountain with snow in the interior of Deltanos? If so, you could practice there."

After a moment of reflection, Prince Samuel replied, "Yes, we do, Nonna Maria. In fact, there is a mountain range similar to these on Fain Island, off the coast. Fain is wild, uninhabited and largely unexplored. Perhaps we could create a toboggan run there as well. I would like that a great deal."

The group paired off into their assigned teams, gathered their toboggans, and headed over to the furthest run on the left.

While they were walking, Alphonse spoke about the toboggan. "Toboggans have been used for centuries, my friends. No one knows exactly where they originated, but I imagine our ancestors first used toboggans to bring game home over long distances when they went hunting. They would secure their kill on the toboggan and pull it, for the toboggan's smooth, flat bottom would glide with little effort over snow and ice. Perhaps they started using them for pleasure when hunters found themselves facing a long, snowy slope and decided to climb aboard and ride down, rather than walk."

"Tobogganing is a fun and exhilarating sport, but the potential for danger exists if it is not done skillfully. The device works like this: Leaning your body the direction you want to travel makes the toboggan turn, but only gradually, so you must anticipate your turns. Balance is the key. The person in the front will be the helmsman and the person in the back must lean in the direction that the helmsman leans."

Prince Solomon asked, "However does one stop such a device, Alphonse? There is no anchor. It would seem to me that a toboggan in motion would surely tend to stay in motion."

Snickers and laughter accompanied Francisco answer to Solomon's question. "There are a few ways to slow and stop, *amigo*. One is to put your feet out and drag them on the snow. Another is to turn the toboggan sideways but lean to the opposite side of the turn and let the snow's resistance slow your ride.

He grinned, "Probably the most undesirable way to stop is to hit something that doesn't move, but most persons choose the other methods."

The group laughed and then gathered into a loose circle. Francisco, then Alphonse led the group in a brief prayer asking the Lord for a safe but fun afternoon.

When the prayer was over, Alphonse donned his helmet and urged the others to do the same. He grinned mischievously and said to Francisco, "Will you be sure to tell Chantal that I am wearing my helmet, old chap? She gave this one to me as a gift, and although I don't really think wearing this gear is necessary, I shall honor my promise to her. She worries so. And you should do the same. Mirna worries about you too."

Francisco nodded and donned his helmet as well. "*Sí, amigo*. And I think that for now on I shall do as *mi esposa*, my wife, asks in this matter. Perhaps this really is necessary. *Y tu, amigo*. You, too, my friend. From now on, we should both wear our helmets. Deal?"

Alphonse nodded in agreement. "Deal. I suppose we are not really invincible after all. Well, not anymore, *amigo*."

Francisco grinned then paused and looked at Alphonse. He said wistfully, "Alphonse, someday perhaps you will learn Spanish, the world's language of vivid color and deep emotions."

Noticing the surprised look on Alphonse's face, Francisco hastily continued, "Not that English is bad, *amigo*; English is a perfectly fine language. But I think God gave us the Spanish language for a reason – for us to truly express ourselves with the rich, full flavor of our meanings."

A slow smile spreading across his face, Alphonse started to speak but was interrupted by Francisco, who laughed and said, "*Amigo*, you should hear the Scot speak Spanish. He makes himself understood, but barely. *Madre Dios*, does he mangle the accent."

Both Alphonse and Francisco burst into laughter. Francisco, still chuckling, waved and jogged back to the others and saying, "*Amigos y amiga*, shall we be on our way?"

With a nod, Ayres walked back to his sleigh and started down the hill.

Penn, Peel, and Ayres had drawn straws to see who would ride first on the toboggan and the sleigh. Peel had drawn the long straw and so was the first to ride the toboggan; Ayres had offered to make the first sleigh ride down the hill to retrieve the riders.

Penn had walked back to Squeaky and was in earnest conversation with another member of the Board of Entry.

As Alphonse and Nonna Maria sat on their toboggan waiting for the others to get ready, Nonna Maria turned back toward Alphonse, and said with a broad smile, "Ah, yes, I remember the toboggan, Alphonse. I recall many happy moments in my childhood playing in the snow with my brothers and sisters."

Alphonse said, "We have a few minutes. I have always wanted to get to know you better, Nonna Maria. Tell me about your childhood. Was winter in Tuscany much different than here in Tierary?"

A faraway look came over her face as she continued, "No, Alphonse, not really. Like here, the family was, and still is, the main focal point in life. My family farms for a living and the coming of the cold seasons meant time off to relax and prepare for the warmer times to come. Winter was always a time to do indoor chores like making and mending clothes, tools, tallow candles and the like. We sang songs and enjoyed each other's company. The growing times were fun but winter was the most enjoyable time for my family, probably because we had much more free time. Ah, yes, winter was fun.

Tobogganing, making snow angels, riding sleds, building snow forts and playing 'capture the flag', skating on the ice. I can recall my sisters and me lying in the snow, collecting individual snowflakes on our mittens, marveling at their delicate and intricate patterns, trying to find their exact duplicate. We used to draw them to compare with the others. We made dozens, maybe hundreds of drawings. Never did we succeed." Nonna Maria paused, then said, "Somehow, I don't think that any two snowflakes are the same. And, when you use a magnifying glass to examine similar flakes, the differences are only more pronounced. I think that this is one area that God uses to show how big he is."

Alphonse smiled and nodded in agreement. Just then, Francisco walked over and explained that somehow the tow-rope on Domani had frayed during the journey and needed to be mended.

Francisco said, "Peel and Samuel are working on the matter as we speak. We shall delay but a few moments longer, friends."

Both Alphonse and Nonna Maria smiled and nodded their understanding, and with a shout Samuel called to Francisco that the repair was complete. With a wave, Francisco turned and walked back toward the waiting others. Solomon, Peel and the others were bent over with laughter; Samuel had tried to sit on the toboggan and Peel had pulled it out from underneath him. The circus clown had sat down hard upon the snowy ground and was now rubbing his posterior.

Francisco and Alphonse guffawed as Nonna Maria rolled her eyes, snorted, then smiled, "Slapstick humor, I know, I know. Initiation rites for the new riders. I have several brothers too. I suppose you men never outgrow such foolishness, do you?"

Alphonse and Francisco looked at each other and burst into more laughter.

When he could speak, Alphonse said, "I hope not, Nonna Maria."

Francisco added, "Me either. Time to get back." With a wave, he headed back toward the others.

As Francisco walked away, Nonna Maria added with a sigh, "Men. Well, I for one hope you never do either. Some of the spice of life would be missing."

Then she chuckled, "A very small amount, that is."

Alphonse laughed and said, "Do continue about your childhood, Nonna Maria."

She replied, "Well, Alphonse, we used to build people of snow and decorate them with old clothes and toy jewelry. One day we built an excellent replica of our papa in the front yard. We pulled his hat down low on his head, over his face. Then it started to snow hard, blizzard conditions almost, and old Mr. Ciccarelli, the town cobbler, happened to be walking by."

"He stood at the fence and yelled at our snow papa to get out of the weather. Even with his thick spectacles on he couldn't see that well and we laughed and laughed from inside our warm, snug home. Mama had Papa bundle up and go out into the storm to Mr. Ciccarelli and explain that he was yelling at Papa's snow double."

"They both roared with laughter and Papa invited him in for dinner. He accepted and after that became a close friend of the family. My brother, Nico, went to work for him soon afterwards and eventually took over his business when Mr. Ciccarelli retired. You know, come to think of it, I never did learn his first name. He, and all adults, were only to be addressed by Mister or Missus and then their last name as a sign on respect.

Then, later they would be addressed by their surname, if they allowed it."

Alphonse commented, "God is good, isn't He? I can tell that you had a great childhood."

Nonna Maria paused and recalled, "Yes, but like Solomon's, my parents were rather strict. Loving but strict. They would give us the good things that they could, but they required good behavior in return. And that we complete our chores before having any free time for ourselves. On snowy days outside I can still remember Mama bringing us thick, hot coca in steaming mugs with tiny, melting marshmallows floating on top. Our lips would be frozen and we could feel the warm cocoa going down our throats to warm our very insides. Of course, that was *after* the walks were cleared of snow and ice."

She sighed, "Yes, I had a good childhood, Alphonse. And more than anything I want such happiness for the children of the Angel School. Sophie should do well there, she will be safe and protected. I'm glad I came across her."

Alphonse said gently, "Indeed, and I as well. Especially as I leave my position and have much more time on my hands. Our new business will be quite lucrative and once established should free even more time for us all." He looked up and saw the others getting into position on their toboggans and said, "Well, that was a quick fix. The others are about ready. Shall we be on our way? I always like to be the leader."

Nonna Maria nodded her assent. Alphonse gave the toboggan a small push and climbed on as the device slowly picked up speed and started down the run. At first the slope was gentle and the ride easy. The run then forked left and right; a bright yellow sign attached to a tree in the middle announced that choosing the right fork allowed the rider to merge over to the more difficult run on the right. Choosing the left fork would continue on the easier run. Alphonse made a split second decision and steered the toboggan to the right. In the blink of an eye, they were speeding down the hill, and Nonna Maria let out a yelp of delight.

For the barest of moments, Alphonse allowed the toboggan to reach maximum speed and then guided Domani to a gentle halt at the first rest stop.

Nonna Maria hugged Alphonse, as both were laughing with the joy of the ride.

Rikkita, ridden by Francisco and Solomon, and Rebecca, ridden by Prince Samuel and Peel had followed the first riders and soon joined the waiting two sitting on the toboggan, enjoying the others coming down the hill.

Prince Solomon let out an excited whoop, and everybody laughed.

Prince Samuel looked at the members of the Lionhearted Club and exclaimed, "Amazing. What a thrill. What great sport. And these are the easiest runs of them all. Francisco, you were right with your description of Rebecca. We hit a bump and I think that we were even flying for a few moments. Hmmm. I wonder how the furthest run on the right could be?"

Alphonse grinned, "Well, then, let's finish this run and work our way to the right." With a shout and a shove, he and Nonna Maria were on their way, followed in hot pursuit by the other two toboggans in an exciting race to the bottom.

22
Chapter Twenty Two
The Boutoy

About the same time the three toboggans were racing down the hill, Andrew stirred, opened his eyes and sat up with a yawn.

Chantal, Crestina and Angeline sat attentively as Mirna said casually to Andrew, "Good afternoon, sleepyhead."

Andrew looked around for a moment and said with difficulty, "Where is Papa?"

Mirna smiled and said, "They are on the Hill. You fell asleep in Squeaky, and rather than wake you, we brought you here. Do you remember the sleigh ride to *La Casita*?"

Puzzled, Andrew shook his head and replied, "No."

Mirna handed Andrew his horn, gestured to Angeline and said, "In time, you will. Andrew, I want you to meet Angeline, your new speech and stretching teacher. She is Crestina's sister."

Angeline brushed back a strand of shoulder length blonde hair, leaned forward and extended her hand. In her musical French accent, she said, "So good to meet you, Andrew. I have heard so many nice things about you from Crestina."

Andrew shyly extended his own hand to meet Angeline's. "ou're etty."

The ladies laughed and, slightly blushing, Angeline responded, "Thank you. And you are handsome, too, my little sugar plum."

Embarrassed, but still holding her hand, Andrew turned away, the bright crimson on his cheeks complimenting the grin on his face.

Sensing his discomfort, Angeline said gently, "I think we shall become good friends. In fact, I have a surprise for you. A gift."

Andrew let go of her hand and shifted on the couch, looking for the gift.

Angeline laughed, "My, you are an eager little pumpkin, aren't you?" She turned to the others and asked, "Will you please bring the box in here?"

Crestina and Chantal rose from their chairs and then returned, each carrying an end of the large, ornate box.

Andrew honked his horn twice, but Angeline shushed him by placing her finger on her lips. She then reached over and took the horn away from the boy. Andrew's eyes grew wide and a crestfallen, hurt look came over his face. A tear rolled down his cheek.

Angeline smiled and said, "*Mon Cherie*, if you are to learn to speak properly, you must learn to express yourself in a different way. The horn sometimes, *oui*. But other ways, too. But do not worry your handsome face.

Andrew blushed again and Angeline continued "Here is your present, Andrew. I designed this myself, and I believe my gift to you is just what you need at this time. The present is spelled b-o-u-t-o-y, and pronounced 'bow-toy'. Can you spell it with me? Take your time, *Cherie*."

Twice Angeline slowly sounded out and spelled the word as Andrew struggled to copy Angeline's sounds. Finally, efforts dwindling as he grew tired, she held up her hand and indicated that he should stop.

The smile on Angeline's face grew as Andrew shook his head, closed his eyes, and, unbidden, laboriously sounded out the word one more time. He added, "An I ill alk une ay oo."

Exhausted, the boy collapsed back into Mirna's arms, a victorious grin creasing his face. Angeline held Andrew's horn overhead and honked the noisemaker in celebration as the laughing Chantal and Crestina hugged the boy.

Angeline said, "What a marvelous, stupendous effort, Andrew. I am proud of you. And now the time has come to open your gift. You rest and gather your strength. We shall remove the pretty coverings for you."

Andrew shook his head side to side, leaned forward and placed his wrists on top of the beautiful box. He wiggled a thumb and forefinger, a movement that was not lost on Angeline, and looked up at Mirna and said, "omma?"

In an instant Mirna understood, and with a big smile, started unwrapping the box.

Chapter Twenty Three
For the Thrill of the Ride

*T*he wind had picked up in velocity again, and large snowflakes were beginning to join their fellows already covering the ground. This time, the riders agreed there would be no letup. To the informed eye, an abundant snowfall would soon blanket the Hill, accumulating, perhaps, as high as a tall man's waist.

Their day on the hill completed, the friends had joined several junior members of the Board of Entry preparing tea and enjoying some treats courtesy of Alphonse and the Royal Confectionery. *Mañana* Hill was deserted; almost all of the others had decided that in front of the warm hearths in their homes was now where they wanted to be.

A mug of steaming Oolong tea in one hand and a dark chocolate Mango Squeeze truffle in the other, Samuel turned to Alphonse and said, "Alphonse, what do you say that we take just one more run. Just you and me, for the thrill of the ride? We can meet the others at the bottom and go to La Casita from there."

Alphonse set down his mug of hot-peppered liquid chocolate, took one more bite of his delicate caramel and coffee-flavored pastry and grinned at Samuel. He said, "I say, old chap, I think we have made a tobogganeer out of you. One more ride?

I doubt it, but let us ask Penn, Peel and Ayres. Every other senior member from the Board of Entry has gone home. Therefore, they are the final authority on the Hill." He turned to Francisco and said, "What do you think, Francisco? One more run?"

Francisco chuckled and said, "No, *amigo*, my day is over." He peered up at the sky then said seriously, "But if you are to go again, you must go soon. I think that the wind will soon rise and bring added danger to your run."

Penn and Peel were conversing with Ayres as Samuel, Alphonse and Francisco approached with the idea.

After lengthy conversation with the other two members of the Board of Entry, Penn finally returned to Alphonse.

Penn was shaking his head as he approached the two. "Aye, ye can go for one last run. Ordinarily we would say yer daft and refuse, but we took into consideration yer Lionheart status, Alphonse, and yer athleticism, Samuel." He paused, looked Alphonse and Samuel in the eye and said, "There were no other factors involved in our decision."

Both men nodded.

Penn continued, "Okay then, helmets as usual, and observe all standard rules. I'll ride Rikkita; you two, Domani. One run only, and only on the center run. Alphonse, allow moderate speed, and watch for obstructions."

Samuel nodded, impressed with the emphasis on safety and the gravity of making a toboggan run in marginal conditions. He reached up, clasped Penn on the shoulder and said in a solemn voice, "Penn, thank you for letting us take one last run."

Penn smiled, nodded, shrugged his shoulders and concluded, "Aye, think nothing, future king. I remember my first day on the Hill as well. I, too, wanted to take just one more run."

Penn clapped his hands together and continued, "All right then, make quick time, laddies, the weather is becoming a wee bit of a bother. The warm hearth at *La Casita* is beckoning and I have yet to tend to the horses and sleighs. Wave yer hands to let me know when you are ready. Enjoy yer run. Good fortune be with ye."

The Scot turned and moved off toward the observation lane. Samuel said to Alphonse, "I'm glad that Penn will be with us on this run. Somehow I feel safer with him following behind us."

A serious look on his face, Alphonse nodded. "Me, too."

The merry ching-ching sounds of the sleigh bells soon receded and the only sounds to be heard was the wind through the trees.

Alphonse nodded, smiled, and said again in a louder voice, "Yes, me, too. Yet I suspect that he wanted to take one more run as well. His love for the toboggan is well known. I say, the sleighs are on their way down the Hill. We're committed, then. Right-o, old chap. Just a quick briefing: try to be one with the toboggan, and anticipate the terrain ahead. Lean with me into the turns and don't make sudden moves. As you know from our previous runs, balance and teamwork are the keys to a successful two-man trip."

With Samuel seated in the front, Alphonse turned and signaled to Penn that they were ready. Seated on his toboggan, Penn waved back and with a forward sweeping arm motion, gestured for the two to begin their run.

Alphonse laughed, leaned backward, and patted Samuel on his helmet. He said to Samuel, "For the thrill of the ride, eh, Samuel? Then a thrilling ride this shall be. Let's go."

With a shout, Alphonse pushed the toboggan forward, and in the blink of an eye, Domani was speeding down the

Hill. As the two men rounded the first bend, a sharp dogleg to the left, Alphonse noticed a fallen tree branch on the inside side of the run. He slowed, then swerved to avoid the limb. Domani wavered for a moment as Alphonse and Samuel both leaned in opposite directions. Samuel realized his error and leaned the same way as Alphonse, allowing the toboggan to track toward the right. In a flash, the tree branch passed. The toboggan slowed as run flattened out and, laughing, Alphonse shouted above the wind, "Well done, Samuel. Nice recovery. Ready for the next drop?"

Samuel partially turned back to Alphonse, grinned and said, "Thanks. What happens if we hit one?"

Alphonse grinned, "Old man, a small branch like that wouldn't cause too much trouble. I say, a large limb is cause greater concern. Probably nothing good though. Ha. Here comes the second part of the course. All right now. Expect a hard, quick turn to the right, followed by a serpentine turn back to the left, then a sharp drop back to the right and a fast run to the finish. We will quickly develop tremendous speed. This is the dangerous part of the run. Ready? Okay now, here we go. Lean right."

Alphonse and Samuel shifted body weight as one, and the toboggan went into a tightly banked turn to the right. Centrifugal force caused Samuel's left foot to slip off the toboggan and dig deeply into the snow. In an instant, the craft wavered and went out of control. Like a disoriented animal trying to escape an attacking predator, Domani spun clockwise, then rode sideways as she entered the serpentine turn. She then flipped and catapulted both Samuel and Alphonse from the toboggan.

Samuel landed hard and slid up the embankment, finally coming to rest wedged between a fallen log and a mulberry shrub. Spitting out a mouthful of bloody snow, with a groan he grabbed his ribs and right leg.

Alphonse flew headlong through the air, somehow managing to twist his body and extend his arms in front of him, deflecting the blow as his helmeted head struck the trunk of a majestic pine tree with a solid thunk. He cried out in pain, then collapsed into a heap; dark red blood poured from a huge, deep gash on his forehead right under his now-battered helmet.

Penn watched the mishap from his vantage point several toboggan-lengths downhill from the turn. Seeing Samuel's foot slip, he had already grabbed a Fast Help Now kit, risen from his perch, hurdled the railing and was several steps approaching the turn as the mishap occurred.

Samuel waved off the advancing Penn, saying that Alphonse needed his attention instead.

As the Scot neared, Alphonse sat up, moved his arms and legs then managed a weak grin. "My head hurts but I can move my arms and legs and I think I'm going to sleep, and my, how this snow is cold and I sure would like a ride home to see my chums. When is tea time, Duncan?"

Penn managed a grin of his own as he carefully immobilized Alphonse's neck with a brace of woven wicker, then even more carefully removed Alphonse's helmet. He pressed a thick compress bandage on Alphonse's bloody forehead then wrapped another cloth around the injured man's head to keep the compress in place. He repeated the procedure. "Me name's Penn, laddie. Duncan they killed long ago to set an example for the rest of us. Aye, yer a mess, man. Delirious too, but methinks ye may yet recall this conversation. I'll tie ye to Domani and ride with Samuel on Rikkita nice and slow like down the hill. Don't ye move any more. I'll be right back with the second medical kit and have the both of ya down the hill for proper medical attention. Yer hurt badly, man. I've seen wounds like this before in the Far Away War. And whatever ye do, don't close yer eyes. Stay with us, laddie; don't succumb to sleep. No, man that just will not do." Penn grinned, "I'll give ya style points for yer flight, but yer landin' needs some improvement." Both men chuckled and Alphonse started whistling his favorite traveling tune and talking to his pet horse. Penn turned back toward Samuel.

Penn was halfway to the future king when Alphonse grabbed his head and pitched forward in the snow. Writhing with pain, he wound up on his laying on his left side, in a fetal position. He vomited, then again. Through bleary, sideways eyes he watched the former prisoner of war heading toward Samuel. Searing waves of hot pain coursed through Alphonse's head and neck, causing him to scream with agony.

More waves of nausea overcame Alphonse and he pushed himself up on his left elbow to get away from his spew. Reality seemed to ripple and flicker. When the feeling had subsided, he again looked toward his rescuer, who had slowed to a stop several dozen yards away.

To his astonishment, Penn the Scot was now on a smoky battlefield, dressed in full Scottish battle garb, holding a bloody two-handed Norse battle-axe in one massive hand; in the other a mace with a bloodstained spiked ball on a chain dangled at the ready. Floppy, skin-colored bits of something were stuck on some of the spikes. The Scot, splattered with crimson, was standing over a cruelly vanquished foe, savagely looking for another to attack. Tears of rage and bravery rolled down his face, further smearing the gore, as he howled an ancient Gaelic war cry. Alphonse could hear the sounds of explosions, bugles, men shouting in fear, pain, and confusion.

Also audible were the cries of horses screaming in terror. The staccato crackle of musket fire mixed with the sickening, wet sounds of steel and lead shot piercing, tearing, and gouging human flesh. Somehow the acrid smell of gunpowder and the coppery stink of blood filled his nostrils. From far away, a man's screaming drew his attention and dimly Alphonse realized that it was his own voice. Then his eyes rolled backwards and he was mercifully enveloped in velvety blackness.

Sophie sat upright in bed, her face blotchy and contorted with fever's ravage. Her limbs started to shake uncontrollably, and her eyes rolled back. Yelli called a servant to cushion her head, guide her arms, but not restrain the child. Another servant, a man new to her staff, asked if he could get his instruments to bloodlet the girl. Infuriated, Yelli told him to gather his belongings and leave the premises, that under no circumstances would she *ever* let that happen to *any* child or adult under her charge and how *dare* he recommend such a barbaric practice. In response to Yelli's fierce protection, Sophie calmed somewhat. Slowly her tremors faded, but her fever remained high. The nurse gathered the girl up in her arms and shooed the other servants out of the room. With tears spilling down her beautiful mocha-colored cheeks, Yelli prayed, sang gospel hymns from her native Mali, and rocked the girl in a rocking chair. The back-and-forth rhythm seemed to comfort her patient – as it had with the infant Andrew. In the wee hours of the morning Sophie's fever broke; around breakfast time a servant girl found the nurse and patient still in the chair, sleeping soundly.

Alphonse started screaming as the Scot hurried to retrieve the second Fast Help Now kit from Domani, causing the war veteran to stop, then drop to his knees in the deepening snow. He fell forward, his face disappearing in the powder. After a moment he raised himself to his knees, then lifted his hands toward the Heavens. Sobbing, he cried, "God, I've doubted yer existence for many years. But I've seen things I canna explain nor understand, both on the field of battle and in those amazin' growing-houses so I'll give ye a chance. If yer real, if ye truly exist, and if ye got a miracle left in yer bag o' tricks, then work that trick gently on this man. Take his pain away and heal him." The Scot pleaded, "Please God, he's a good man. Please don't let him die."

Then, almost as an afterthought, he whispered, "Aye, ye know me sufferin as well. Take me pain away too, if ye will."

After a moment, Penn rose, took a big breath, exhaled, and again went about the business of tending to the wounded.

Chapter Twenty Four
After

Slowly, his vision became adjusted to the radiance dazzling his eyes. The most beautiful symphony Alphonse had ever heard permeated each fiber of his body. A short, familiar figure dressed in white walked toward Alphonse and stopped in front of him.

Smiling, the figure lifted his arms and said, "Hello, *Tio* Alphonse. Do you recognize me? I'm me, Andrew."

Alphonse gasped in surprise and embraced the boy. He knelt on one knee and exclaimed, "Andrew. I don't understand what is happening here. This music, I have heard it before, haven't I?"

The lad nodded. "Yes you have. Think back, Uncle."

With a flash of insight and recollection, Alphonse exclaimed, "Yes. It's the tune you always hum, right? Good Heavens. That day when I was reading you the bible. Your melody is the music of angels. An angelic symphony. Are those really angels? It's so peaceful, so beautiful here. Where are we? Is this Heaven?"

Alarmed, Alphonse asked Andrew, "I say, have we died and gone to Heaven? How did you get here? You're still alive, aren't you? I'm not ready to die just yet. I still have things to do. Chantal and the children need me."

Andrew laughed easily and gestured to the room. He said, "No, no, *Tio*, this is not Heaven. As beautiful and as wonderful as this is, what you see and hear now is but a tiny part of God's glory, a speck of sand in the vastness and wonder of all His creation. Heaven is much, much more. Our minds are not capable of grasping all that Heaven is."

Alphonse looked around the room and recognized several children from the Angel School. They waved and Alphonse smiled and waved back. He turned to Andrew and asked, "But why are we here? How are the others from the Angel School here too? How am I here? And you. You have a normal body. The others, too. How marvelous."

Alphonse paused, "I still do not understand. Are you *sure* I'm not dead?"

Andrew smiled, "No, *Tio* Alphonse, you're not dead. You almost were when your ship was fighting Jastin and you were wounded, but no, God has more time on earth for you."

Relieved, Alphonse said, "How many more years, Andrew? No, wait. I don't want to know. It would be a burden too great to bear."

Andrew nodded, "Very wise, *Tio*. You see, God has created our lives on two levels of existence. There is a physical level of what we see, smell, taste, hear and feel with our bodies. With those senses we know the world He has created for us. But there is a spiritual level as well, the level of Heaven, of angels, of the infinite glory of the Trinity. That level is where we are aware of God's nearness. As people grow older, a few remain close to God, but mostly when children with normal bodies grow into adults they gradually become numb to God's presence and glory. They may believe in God, even accept His salvation, but do not live their lives in harmony with Him. God allows them to experience the consequences of their actions to draw them back to Him. Some do, some do not. Others, as they grow older, act in shameful ways, create false gods or even deny His very existence. Some even claim to be gods. Sadly, that belief is on the spiritual level too, only far from the truth."

Andrew laughed. "Silly people. To think *they* could be God or that He does not exist. What foolishness. If they don't return to Him, they will find out the truth in time. Then it will be too late and they will spend eternity in misery away from God. But these children that you see were given different bodies in the physical level, perhaps to let God work through their circumstance and to bring those who come in contact with them back to Him. God alone knows the reason they receive bodies or minds that do not work as others. These children stay close to Him on the spiritual level no matter what age their body becomes. They sometimes see things that most people do not see and sing songs that most people do not hear."

"Their bodies may even sway and keep time with the angels in worshiping God. However it happens, God has shown his love for we little ones in a special way by giving us this gift of enjoying our perfect, Heavenly bodies in advance, especially when we sleep." Andrew concluded with a wry observation, "Many people pity us because we are different, but there are those of us who pity those who are 'normal' because they cannot enjoy their perfect bodies now as we do."

With a shout, Andrew bounded away, his fluid movements in perfect synchronicity with the intricate ebb and flow of the angelic symphony as the heavenly beings played their instruments and sang praises to the Almighty. All around, Alphonse could see children from the Angel School and many other places from around the world, dancing and singing along with the angels, also praising God and worshiping Him with their voices and dance.

For a long while Alphonse pondered all that Andrew had spoken. He watched the dancing youngsters' joyous interaction with the angels and each other. All at once he felt his hips start to sway to the music and looked down to see his feet tapping time to the beat.

Finally, Andrew approached again and Alphonse said, "But how is it that am I here?"

Andrew responded, "I don't know *why*, *Tio* Alphonse. Perchance the blows to your head in the last few days have something to do with your presence here. But I *do* know that somehow God has permitted you to see angels and into this part of our lives and Penn's wartime experiences as well. Empathy is stronger than sympathy. You have been supportive of the Angel School for many years; now perhaps you can minister to the children with deeper insight and understanding than before."

Alphonse chuckled and said, "Yes, I believe that I can, nephew. This is such a wonderful place. I want to dance, too, and sing, but there are so many more questions that I want to ask–"

At that moment the golden light and angelic music started to whirl, picking up speed and blending together then quickly fading away into the fitful darkness of deep slumber.

After a while, Alphonse felt himself emerging from the twilight of sleep back into the world of men. He stirred and slightly moved his heavily bandaged head. Slowly he opened his eyes to see Chantal's relieved face peering down at him.

His wife's artificially buoyant voice belied the concern evident in her eyes. "Welcome back, dear sir. You've given us quite a fright. How are you feeling?"

Alphonse smiled, reached up and drew his wife close. Through parched lips, he said thickly, "I wore my new helmet."

Chantal picked up his helmet, battered and speckled with dried blood and held it up for his inspection. "I know. Thank you."

Alphonse grinned, "This bandaged old noggin is tougher than any old tree. I say, do you have a spot of tea? I am terribly thirsty."

Tears of relief welled in her eyes and slid quietly down her cheeks as she hugged her husband and said quietly, "I thought I'd lost you, my darling. I haven't left your side since they brought you in." She gently kissed him on the cheek then gave him small sips from a waiting glass of Angeline's special tincture for head injuries.

Alphonse drank eagerly, and Chantal had to slow him down to prevent the cool liquid from spilling down his chin onto the bed. At last his thirst was quenched and the two snuggled together.

Several minutes passed with the two murmuring their love for each other, the tender moment finally passing when Francisco and Mirna entered the room.

Francisco took Alphonse's hand as Mirna sat on the edge of the bed and placed her hand on top of Francisco's.

The elder's voice was tinged with relief and exhaustion, "Alphonse. You're awake. *Bienvenidos, amigo.* Welcome back, my friend. Praise to God in Heaven for answering our prayers. We haven't slept a wink since you tried to knock the pine tree down with your head three days ago. Samuel has a deep bruise on his arm, cracked rib and a twisted knee. And he has a banged up face, too. How are you feeling?"

Before Alphonse could answer, the room was suddenly filled with Samuel, Solomon, Nonna Maria, Crestina, Angeline,

Penn, Peel and Ayres. Everybody spoke at once, echoing Francisco, Mirna and Chantal.

Slowly, Alphonse raised his hand to quell the bedlam, smiled and said weakly, "I am fine, just tired. I am happy to see you all, my friends. I am going to be fine. Thank you for all your prayers. Samuel, are you all right? I remember you flying up in the air and landing up the embankment on the fallen log...and Penn... ."

Prince Samuel limped meekly to the bedside. The bandages on his face and the sling on his arm stood in mute testimony to his not-so-happy landing. He said, "Alphonse, I am deeply sorry for causing the accident. My foot slipped off of the toboggan and then we crashed."

Alphonse said, "I disagree, Samuel. The accident was not your fault. We should not have gone so fast into the right turn. That was my mistake. But praise God, Penn the Scot was there, eh, old chap? Things might have turned out differently without him. I say, we shall tackle the center run again, and conquer it next time. Can you still perform at the circus?"

Samuel shrugged, "Future performances remain to be seen, Alphonse. Probably not for the children of the Angel School; yet, the circus is more than just one performer. The show must go on."

He smiled, then winced as a cut on his lip reopened and a drop of blood trickled down to his chin. "Oops. This is more painful than my other injuries." He blotted his lip with a clean cloth. "In fact, I have asked Penn to be the honorary Grand Marshal for the parade. And you must accompany him as well, Sir Alphonse the Lionheart." Everybody laughed and he continued, "I must be getting back for preparations. I wanted to stay and pray for your recovery and to apologize in person."

Alphonse smiled and the two men shook hands; one in forgiveness extended, the other in forgiveness received.

Samuel brightened, pointed at his ribs and said, "The past two days have been quiet as we have prayed for you without ceasing. Happily, the mood has lightened now that you have regained consciousness. Although I am glad you are feeling better, I soon stand to be in great pain."

Everybody laughed again and, one by one, expressed get-well wishes.

Penn was the last to stop by Alphonse's bed. Taking Alphonse's hand in his own, Penn smiled and said gently, "Welcome back, laddie. My prayers have been answered. Get better soon so we can work on yer landin' style."

Both men laughed at their private joke and Alphonse murmured his thanks. "Penn, you're a hero. No, you are a hero *again*. You saved my life. Thank you."

Chantal joined her husband and together both expressed thanks for Penn's cool headedness and skill in dealing with Alphonse's injuries.

Tears of joy running down his face, the Scot squeezed Alphonse's hand with his massive hand, then turned away. He said softly, "T'wern't nothin', laddie. T'wern't nothin' a'tall. I'm just happy that yer going to be okay."

Penn took a deep breath and turned back towards Alphonse. Tears welled up in his eyes. "I'm going to be okay too, Alphonse. These past three days I have had long, deep conversations with Francisco, Mirna, Nonna Maria, Samuel and Solomon.

They have introduced me to the Lord Jesus and I have accepted His salvation. Aye, what burdens were lifted from me back, mon. Memories of The Far Away War are no longer painful. Now I am truly free."

Alphonse smiled, "There are no surprises with God, Penn. Somehow I heard and saw and smelled your battle experience. You had a mace and a battle axe. Perhaps all this happened to me so you may have some time with your soon-to-be brothers and sisters in the Lord. If so, I would gladly pay the price again."

Penn murmured, "Maybe so, laddie, maybe so. God works in mysterious ways."

There wasn't a dry eye in the room as finally, Nonna Maria shushed the group and herded the visitors out of the room. She, Chantal, Mirna and Angeline then removed the bandages from Alphonse's head. In the middle of his forehead was a large ugly purple knot and deep gash, which elicited a gasp from Francisco, who had taken one last look over his shoulder as he was walking out the doorway.

"*Amigo*, you have three eyes." Francisco said with a grin, and came back to Alphonse's bedside. He took Alphonse's hand in his own, lowered his voice and said, "I am happy that you are going to be fine, my friend. Rest, and we shall see you in the morning. *Huevos rancheros* for breakfast?"

Alphonse laughed and responded in a weak voice, "*Sí, amigo. Con salsa picanté y guacamole y tortillas. Por suprestro, con café y leche y azucar, tambien.*"

Mouth agape, Francisco stared at Alphonse. Finally, he snorted and said with a grin, "With picanté sauce and *guacamole* and *tortillas*? With coffee and cream and sugar also? Consider the matter done. Alphonse, not only have we turned your taste buds into those of a regular Spanish gentleman, but now you speak our language as well. Is that all you must do to learn a new language? Bash a tree? Use your head as a battering ram? I have been covertly trying to teach you Spanish for years now. I must be an excellent teacher."

Chantal explained that in the last few months she and Alphonse had engaged a special tutor to learn Francisco and Mirna's native tongue and were waiting for the opportune moment to surprise their friends.

"We almost spilled the beans at the Gingerbread House, and again on *Mañana* Hill, Francisco. I'm happy that we didn't. The look on your face just now was priceless," said Alphonse.

The still-chuckling Francisco said, "Now I am certain that you're going to be fine, *amigo*," waved goodbye and left to share the anecdote with the others.

Mirna, Nonna Maria and Angeline gently cleaned and reapplied healing balm to the wound then re-bandaged Alphonse's head. After expressing their relief to Alphonse they slipped from the room.

In quiet tones, husband and wife murmured their love for each other.

Alphonse suddenly looked at Chantal and said with alarm, "Where is Andrew? Is he going to be all right? I saw him—"

Placing a gentle finger on his lips, Chantal quieted her husband, saying, "You saw him only in your dreams, dearest. Our Sing Song Child is sleeping in his chambers. He woke up shortly after you and the rest of you adventurers left for *Mañana* Hill. Andrew has been awake and acting his usual self these past days. Crestina brings him in often to check on you, despite Mirna's wishes to leave you be."

The fog of fatigue started enveloping Alphonse. Eyes drooping, he said thickly, "Can he talk again? Chantal, I spoke with him. Yes, he *can* talk."

His wife shook her head and said, "No, not so, dearest, only with great difficulty as before but there is great hope for him. Angeline says that with hard work and perseverance, he could perhaps talk with only a little or maybe no trouble. Remember that large, wrapped box in their sleigh? She brought a tool she designed to help him and others perhaps recover some lost manual dexterity. Angeline calls the device a 'boutoy', and there are twelve different colored sides covered with as many different surfaces—from smooth to soft to rough and so on. There are doors of different sizes to open; each door makes a different sound that Andrew has to imitate. The boutoy is difficult for him to manipulate, but Andrew is a determined boy. He has already spent hours playing with the device, and Angeline says that maybe in a year or so with hard work he could have almost normal use of his arms and legs. Speech too. Good news indeed. He is a motivated and determined boy who is growing fast into a very motivated and determined young man."

Chantal paused and looked at her husband, who looked back at her through almost closed eyelids.

She chuckled and said, "Okay, enough about the boutoy. I can relax now that you are going to be fine. Go back to sleep, dearest. I will be back later in a few hours, and in the morning you will be stronger. We can go home to *La Estancia* the day after tomorrow."

Chantal looked at the almost asleep figure and said, "I will continue to pray for you, my love, but right now I am going to go to the kitchen for some dinner. I'm famished."

She kissed his lips gently, rose from the bed and with a caress of his cheek, turned and left the room.

Alphonse smiled and drifted back to a deep, restful sleep. Later, he awoke to find Andrew napping on top of the bed covers nestled close, head upon Alphonse's chest.

A single candle protected by a crystal globe illuminated the room. Laughter and tantalizing smells from the kitchen drifted up the staircase. The season's first Torrie Rose rested in dusky red majesty from a delicate porcelain vase on the nightstand. Andrew stirred and peered up at his uncle, then smiled his lopsided grin as the elder grinned back.

Alphonse croaked, "Well hello, Andrew. I guess Crestina broke the rules again. I'll have to thank her in the morning. I'm glad that you're better." He yawned and felt the tug of sleep overtaking him. "I must know, old chap. Tell me, was it real or was it all a dream?"

Andrew smiled, laid his head back down on his uncle's chest and softly hummed a gentle, nameless, but now familiar melody. Alphonse immediately recognized the little boy's little tune as the tip of an iceberg, a minuscule part of an intricate and eternal angelic symphony.

Doubts erased, Alphonse lay back and drifted off to sleep, hand in hand with the Sing Song Child as they walked toward the warm, golden light and the music of angels.

The End

Epilogue

One day after the group returned to *La Estancia*, a carriage accompanied by armed riders left the main building and pulled out towards the gate and the Angel School. Over to the side, a boy with crude metal braces on his legs stood with the help of two manservants. When the helpers let go of his arms, the boy took a hesitant step forward, lost his balance, and fell face down. He spat out a piece of dirt. Blood trickled from his nose and he grunted in frustration. Tears welled up in his eyes and flowed down his grimy face as pushed himself up to see the carriage. His eyes locked with those of one of the passengers, an adolescent golden haired girl.

His heart fluttered, as did hers.

The girl's heart now bursting with joy, rubbed away an imaginary splotch of dirt from her nose then smiled and waved. The boy smiled his lopsided smile and slowly raised his hand.

The carriage rounded a bend and was lost from view.

"See you next week in the Angel School, Sophie," he said softly and slowly, each word *perfectly articulated*.

After about half an hour's travel the carriage slowed to pass a tall peasant boy on the shoulder of a narrow part of the road. Something about the shape of the boy's head was familiar to the girl, and she leaned out the window for a better look.

"RHYS it's YOU" she cried, and the carriage's other passenger, Yelli the head nurse, had to restrain her from leaping out the window.

"Sophie?" the boy answered as he started running alongside. "Sophie. It's *you*. Oh my, it's really *YOU*. We thought you were dead. What are you doing in the carriage? Oh, we have bad news. Stepfather's been killed."

The carriage slowed to a stop. The boy climbed in the carriage and after a brief discussion Yelli issued new directions to the driver and guards.

Soon the carriage pulled in front of Sophie's former home. Her mother and siblings were overjoyed at her return and bombarded her with questions. In due time, Sophie learned that the morning after she was thrown out, an angry bull gored Stepfather in the stomach and it's horn pulled out some of his intestines. Uncharacteristically going to aid the wounded man, the earl was trampled, and gored in the chest before Rhys and another of her brothers could distract the animal away. Stepfather died shortly afterwards and was buried on the hill behind the barn.

The earl now lay gravely injured inside the hovel, unable to be moved to his castle.

His voice came weakly from inside, asking for Sophie. She went through the doorway and was startled to see him lying propped up on Mother and Stepfather's bed. Once a great hulk of a man, the earl now appeared gray, shrunken and weak. The sickly foul stench of runaway infection and unwash was upon him and although the day was cool, there was a hot sheen of perspiration on his brow.

He was dying.

Sophie shrank back, afraid. The earl beckoned her closer; woodenly, she obeyed. He took her hand and she was repulsed by his smell. His doctor had bled him and introduced maggots to his wound to devour the infected flesh, but to no avail. With tears streaming from his eyes, he begged her to forgive him for his wickedness towards her family in the past. Stunned, she just stood there. He continued in a raspy voice just louder than a whisper, "Those two armed men standing guard outside the barn told me to change my ways and not to bother you or anyone else again." Gagging, he gasped for breath. "When I reached for my dagger they drew their swords, the brightest and sharpest I've ever seen. They pointed them at me. They shouldn't have been bright, it was night, but they were bright as the sun. I was so frightened that when I came to my senses I turned right around and came back into the house."

Mother gave him a sip of ale and wiped his brow. "I did. I examined my life. Right there in the dark of the night in this very bed I became aware of my wickedness and with all my heart asked God to forgive me. He did; I know this, and I was determined to turn from my ways. After we were injured by the bull, I knew your Stepfather and me were going to die." He coughed. "I resolved to take care of your family, so I deeded this farm, the land around it and the land you were working the day you were thrown out, to your brother and family. It's been lawfully recorded and I paid the land tax in advance for seven years. You and your family are now landowners, owners of everything on and in it. Use it wisely."

He coughed again, this time harder and Sophie could see frothy red spittle on his lips. She pulled away. He groaned and shifted; his blanket fell away, revealing a bandage crusty with seepage and dried blood. Something pulsed under his exposed skin, and she threw up a little in her mouth. Mother repositioned the blanket.

Sophie looked at him. "But earl, I didn't have any guards. I'm just a poor peasant girl."

Struggling for breath he shook his head and wheezed, "No, no, I saw them, and they changed my life. I am sorry for all that has happened to you and your family. Somehow I knew you were coming back today and so I've waited. I am a stubborn old man. Please forgive me, as God has."

She moved closer. "Of course I forgive you, earl. I really do."

A faraway look came into his eyes and color came into his face. He seemed a little stronger. "Thank you. Now, legend holds that somewhere on my land–your land now–is supposed to be a lost Roman treasure. Lost for over a thousand years. Since I was a wee lad I've looked for it. My entire life."

The earl stiffened and gasped as a bolt of pain coursed through his body. Suddenly he looked upwards, his grimace turning into a weak smile. "Oh my. What's that? Can you hear the music? Can you?"

She shook her head. "Music? No, I can't."

"How beautiful. I hear … it's a symphony unlike any I've ever heard. It's lovely beyond belief. I can see your bodyguards … brighter than the sun … see them … see your father … he's smiling and welcoming me … gold … yes."

His gaze fixed at a point far beyond the ceiling and his chest fell one last time. After a few minutes Rhys stepped forward and closed his eyes.

For a long while the house was quiet.

A partridge sounded in the distance, breaking the silence. Without thinking, Sophie tried to trick it into returning her call. Success.

Sophie pressed a silver coin and a broken piece of pottery into the palm of his lifeless hand. A tear rolled down her cheek as she curled his fingers closed.

She whispered, "Godspeed, earl. You've found your treasure after all."

Author's Notes

Some folks ask where I 'got' my inspiration for the plot and characters in my book...the short answer is from God.

It's true, and all praise goes to Him. But that doesn't quite explain the nuts and bolts. You see, I travel often and I meet a lot of people. A lot. Just a few make an impression on me. Fewer still become characters in my stories.

For example, I met **Nonna Maria** in a hotel lobby one hot summer day. As we chatted I discovered she's a true to life hero just as I described in The Sing Song Child. Nonna Maria's an elementary school administrator from the poorer side of town completely dedicated to her students.

The Sing Song Child is real, albeit a victim of autism (I think) — not a virus. I met him in a crowded Las Vegas airport food court. A co-worker, Tammy, and I watched a boy follow his mother through the crush of humanity as if tethered at the waist by a thick, invisible rope. Nothing could have stopped him from following her. As he walked, **Andrew** had his left arm extended straight in front of him, bent perpendicular at the elbow. His hand was flat and held high in the air...his right arm covered his midsection. His head was swaying from side to side in a peculiar rhythmic motion. I remarked that it looks like he's keeping time to music only he can hear. Tammy said yeah, the music of angels...I said maybe he is...

(Mike) **Penn**, (Tim) **Ayres and** (Bob) **Peel** are real life colleagues I *greatly* respect and admire. Your courage and sacrifice for our nation is an inspiration for us all. Thank you, thank you, thank you. You will never be forgotten. Mr. Penn can be reached at **www.captainmikepenn.com**

Yelli? The nickname of a gracious and wonderful woman named Danielle who was immensely helpful one difficult time not too long ago. I met **Crestina**, **Angeline** and **Teresa** -three sisters traveling together- on a flight one day. Nice ladies all, thanks for your encouragement... you're in my book, as promised. Thank you to my family (Vicki, Ryan, Rachel and Caralina) for your love and encouragement during this whole process. **Tierary** is a compilation of my children's names. **Tie** comes from my youngest daughter, **Caralina**. When she was a little baby no longer than my forearm I'd hold her and call her my 'tiny girl'. One day, to my surprise she said 'Tie Tie'. **Ra** comes from my eldest daughter **Rachel**, and **Ry** is from my son **Ryan**. TieRaRy. I love you all *more*. The town of 'Vittoria' and 'Torrie Roses' in all their beauty, splendor and majesty are named after my wife, **Vittoria (Vicki)**. Love you, honey.

I've taken extensive literary license in my story. Chantal and Mirna's 16th century genius in creating and morphing Chañisós and Chasalotés from ordinary plants will need to stay between them and God, but He gets the glory always. Alphonse's crafting a 'wheeled chair' and 'rocking chair' centuries before they were created also begs your forgiveness. But yes, there really is such a thing as a potato shovel. Some folks ask 'why 1574'? Well, those were much simpler times. I researched (and researched) for clothes, food, transportation, and the myriad aspects of life so long ago. Amazingly, a great deal of information exists, and what I didn't know or couldn't find...I made up. Literary license.

To my very special encourager and dear friend, **Betty Rosentrater**, a big, big hug for you.

'Thank You' goes to my immensely patient editor, **Thornton Sully**, of **A Word With You Press**. Thanks too, to **Joseph (Joe) DeSantis**, my father-in-law, for his encouragement early on in this book's infancy. **Barbara Roberts Pine**...you saw my story's potential. Fellow writer **Michael Stang**, your literary genius has always inspired me to be a better writer.

To the awesome **Flight Attendants, Pilots, ground employees and Colleen Barrett of the LUV Airline**, THANK YOU for your love and encouragement.

I've enjoyed working with my talented artists **Heather Miller** of Oceanside, California, who designed and drew Penn's Mace and Battle Axe, and the Snowflake...and San Diego's cover/back page artist **Ian Holaday**, who owns Holaday Arts. A writer creates a reality of sorts from their imagination. But what Heather does with a pencil and paper...and Ian does with a stylus on a computer screen...is simply magic.

More about the artists later in this book.

I hope you enjoyed the *Sing Song Child,* and I look forward to sharing more of Andrew's adventures with you in my next book, *The Angel School.*

One last thing: I've always wanted to say hello to my mother **Mary Ann Casper** on a national stage. Hi Mom! I Love You!

My Very Warmest Regards to everyone,
Mike Casper
November 2014

About The Artists:

Ian Holaday has been a digital media artist for well over 6 years with significant knowledge in illustration, design, web and video media. He extends to his clients a wide variety of unique skills to help bring their ideas and imagination to life.

If you have a digital media project in mind, you can find a list of his services at **ianholaday.com**

Heather Miller: "Art has always been a passion of mine. Ever since I was a toddler, I've had professional instruction as well as countless hours of my own practice. To me, art is a way for me to appreciate the beauty in life, fictional or non-fictional, and I hope that in these illustrations you can appreciate that beauty too."

You can reach Heather at **hethmiller30@yahoo.com**

Made in the USA
Middletown, DE
24 December 2022

17524709R00113